Mists of Dark Harbor

Other Five Star Titles
by Clarissa Ross:

Ghost of Dark Harbor
Hearse For Dark Harbor
Dark Harbor Haunting
Secret of the Pale Lover

Mists of Dark Harbor

Dark Harbor Series

#3

Clarissa Ross

Five Star
Unity, Maine

BC

Five Star First Edition Romance Series.

Published in 2001 in conjunction with Maureen Moran Agency.

Set in 11 pt. Plantin by Christina S. Huff.

Printed in the United States on permanent paper.

Library of Congress Cataloging-in-Publication Data

Ross, Clarissa, 1912–
   Mists of Dark Harbor / Clarissa Ross.
      p. cm.—(Dark Harbor series ; bk. 3)
   ISBN 0-7862-2946–2 (hc : alk. paper)
   I. Title.
PR9199.3.R5996 M56 2001
   813′.54—dc21   00-062268

To my friends Fran and George Urqhart,
of Moncton, N.B., Canada

Chapter One

Nina Patton stood leaning against the railing of the Captain's Walk, high atop the old mansion of Blue Gables. She stared beyond the village of Dark Harbor below and studied the broad expanse of blue ocean in the distance. Once again she experienced that feeling of dread which she had known since she had first become a guest at the ancient summer residence of the Carter family.

She had made the journey to Pirate Island for an express purpose, to try and clear the name of the man she loved. For Grant Carter was dead and could no longer defend himself. Yet the political scandal and scurrilous rumors which had been linked to his name before his death had left a blot on his record in public life. And she feared that she was making no progress in clearing his name.

Grant had been on his way to take the ferry from Cape Cod to Pirate Island when a trailer-truck had jackknifed on the road ahead of him and his sports car had shot over a cliff into the ocean. Would-be rescuers had located the car but his body had not been found. The tragic accident had sparked the interest of the newspapers and they began printing all the old accusations against the dead man over again.

Nina knew that the superstitious maintained everyone who lived on Pirate Island for even a short while was likely to fall under its brooding spell. The village which Blue Gables overlooked had gained its name of Dark Harbor as a host to

Puritans, Satanists, pirates, wreckers, smugglers, whalers, hedonists and ordinary fishermen. It was said that those who stayed for a while on the bleak island far out in the Atlantic were never quite the same again. Touched by the grim atmosphere of the fog-shrouded island, they took on a sort of haunted personality.

On this early evening in July the Carters were indulging in that ritual of wealthy summer residents, holding a cocktail party for friends and summer acquaintances. Downstairs in the great paneled living room and outside in the patio by the swimming pool their voices and occasional bursts of laughter could be heard.

Nina had climbed to the roof of the old house to seek out some solitude and enjoy the view from this high point of the island. She was still filled with pain at losing Grant and in no mood for party gaiety. The slight evening breeze rustled her shoulder-length bronze hair, momentarily obscuring her lovely green eyes. Then she brushed the strands back with a slim hand and stared fixedly at the ocean again.

At twenty-four she was at a peak of loveliness. Her V-shaped face was deeply tanned with a faint trace of freckles. Her features were fine, her voice husky and cultured. She played an excellent game of tennis and bridge. Educated at Vassar, she had worked as a welfare agent for more than a year. Then she'd met Grant Carter, fallen in love with him and dedicated her talents to his efforts as a politician.

But now Grant was dead and his political name badly sullied. She was left, rich and unmarried, with only a single purpose in life—to restore Grant's good name. That was why she had come to visit the Carters. But Grant's family and associates showed little interest in her crusade. In fact she sensed open hostility from some of them.

She stood gripping the railing, looking much too beautiful

in a yellow silk pants suit to be dwelling on such somber thoughts. Then she heard a sound behind her and turned to see that a handsome, brown-haired man in a white suit and colorful bow tie had come up to join her.

Nina recognized him at once as Derek Mills, one of the aristocrats of the island and director of the local museum. It was strictly a labor of love, as he was very wealthy. Since the island was only fifteen miles long and three miles wide, gossip was rife among its inhabitants. Nina had heard that Derek Mills had a wife who was mentally ill in a mainland hospital and that there seemed small hope of her recovery. During the previous summer Derek had a love affair with a New York girl which had ended in a sad parting. Nina thought about all this as the young man approached her.

Derek Mills said, "A marvelous view from up here!"

She turned to him with a smile. "Yes."

A look of mild amusement showed on his handsome face. "You're missing the party. Is it deliberate on your part?"

She nodded. "I'm afraid so. I suppose I'm very wicked."

"I wouldn't say that," Derek said. "I became tired of it myself. One has to be in the mood."

"And I'm definitely not."

"I can understand," he said. "You were Grant's fiancée, weren't you?"

"Yes."

"His accident wasn't all that long ago," Derek Mills said. "I remember that he was on the way here when it took place."

"That's the way it was," she agreed.

Derek eyed her thoughtfully. "Grant Carter was running for state district attorney at the time, as I remember."

"You have a reliable memory."

He looked at her hard. "There was a lot of talk."

"There was," she agreed. "I think it must have been

2a

shocking here for Grant's brother and his aunt."

Derek Mills said, "I'm not sure they've minded it all that much. They seem to be having a good time down there now." A burst of laughter and the sounds of accordion music wafted up to them.

Her pretty face took on a frown. "I know. It continually surprises me. No one seems to care too much, except me."

"But I think it's important that someone does," Derek said. "I knew Grant and I liked him. Greg may resemble him in appearance but he'll never match Grant as a human being."

"I'm glad to hear you say that," she exclaimed.

Derek smiled. "I won't say it too loud since Greg is my host. But it is true."

"I've always felt so and I've known them both."

The young man at her side said, "I especially admire your loyalty to Grant in the face of his name being linked with that other woman's."

"Elise Venn?" Nina said. "Her husband is a guest here today. He and the Carter boys were always close friends. Grant's death and Elise's suicide seem not to have changed that."

"Grant never mentioned Elise to me," Derek said.

"Nor to me. I think the scandal was a put-up job," Nina said emphatically.

Derek Mills showed interest. "You do?"

"Yes. I'm sure I would have had some knowledge of it. And Mort Venn has never believed it. The letters that were given to the newspapers were forgeries. But don't ask me how!"

The young man's brown eyes fixed on her. "And you have an idea you can clear Grant's name by coming here to Dark Harbor?"

"I'm convinced some of the people here know facts which

could help solve the mystery."

"But then isn't it possible that his political enemies tried to destroy him?" Derek asked.

"But their campaign was so calculated and diabolical," she protested. "They didn't need to destroy Grant as a man— only to prove he wasn't politically shrewd enough to be the state's district attorney. But they weren't satisfied to stop at that," she finished bitterly.

"And you think you're strong enough to fight such a conspiracy and prove the scandal's a hoax?"

"I hope so," Nina replied. "Perhaps because Grant is dead and everyone else appears to have lost interest. I think some of them may get careless. A word dropped here or there could lead to a solution."

He smiled his appreciation of her words. "I wish you luck. And since I was Grant's friend, consider me yours as well. If you want me at any time, you can generally reach me at the museum or at the house. It's on the road to the monastery."

"Thank you," she said. "I've heard about the monastery. Can you see it from here?"

"Not too well," he said. "It's on the far end of the island. Used to be a leper home at one time. We had to deal with a criminal hippie group who took it over last summer. But we got rid of them."

"I think I heard something about that," she said. She knew that the girl Derek had fallen in love with had been a victim of the hippie cult.

A shadow crossed his handsome face. "No doubt someone has mentioned it," he agreed. "It caused a lot of talk."

"And you have always lived here?"

"Since my college days," he said.

"Don't you feel isolated?"

"No. I'm a true islander. We have ferry service from Cape

Cod and daily plane service during the summer tourist season. We owe our good climate to the proximity of the Gulf Stream. My family dates back to the whaling days when the island was rich and many of the fine old mansions were built, Blue Gables among them."

She said, "I know it must be a very old house."

He nodded. "It was ancient when Grant, Greg and I played here as boys." He glanced at his wristwatch. "I must go. I've promised to meet someone for dinner. I've enjoyed talking with you. We're bound to meet again."

"I hope so," Nina said sincerely. "And I'll not forget your promise of support."

"Don't," he said. And with a final wave and a smile he left her.

She watched him leave with a feeling of regret. Next to Grant, she thought, Derek Mills was perhaps the nicest man she'd ever met. She only wished that Grant's brother Greg had some of his dead brother's charm as well as his looks.

She lingered on the Captain's Walk after the young man left. From time to time she heard goodbyes from below and cars driving away. The party was coming to an end, and a somewhat sullen Greg Carter came up to her rooftop retreat to find her. The good-looking six-footer came striding over to her and exclaimed, "So this is where you hide!"

She turned to look up at the bronzed face, so much like Grant's that it pained her every time they were together. His stern yet even features had a look of youthful strength. But Grant's strength of character was not there.

She said, "I'm sorry, Greg."

"You should be," he said in an annoyed tone. "People were asking for you. Aunt Madge and I had to make excuses. You put us on the spot."

"I didn't mean to."

12

The big man in the plaid jacket and blue trousers said, "I think you did. You blame us for what happened to Grant and you like making us miserable."

"That's not true! How could I possibly blame you for Grant's death?"

"I don't know," Greg said. "But I feel that you do. And so do the others."

"They're wrong!"

"I hope so," Greg said, placing an arm around her. "I thought your coming here would be a good idea. That it might bring us closer together."

"I didn't promise that," she reminded him.

"You didn't promise anything," he admitted. "But I was the one who discovered you first. We were getting along well enough until you met Grant. There's no reason why we can't resume now that Grant is dead."

"No," she said. "I can never offer you more than friendship, Greg."

He frowned. "Why?"

"Too many points to explain," she said. "We'll talk about it some other time."

"I intend that we should," the big, dark-haired man said. "Only the family and regular guests are left now. The housekeeper has a fine buffet set out for us. You'd better come down and have something to eat."

"I don't feel hungry," she protested.

"You will when you see the buffet," Greg said, taking her by the arm and leading her to the stairs.

This overwhelming insistence on Greg's part reminded her of their first meeting. It had been at a party given by one of her girl friends. Greg, the handsome ex-football star, had been the center of attention all that evening. Nina's friend had introduced her to the big man at midevening. And Greg

13

had taken over just as he was doing now.

He had danced with her and taken her out to a balcony where they had their first kiss. He at once set up a series of meetings between them with never a thought that she might not want to see him again. As a matter of fact Nina had been pleasantly impressed by the young man, a successful stockbroker and active playboy. Yet there was something vital lacking in him. She decided it was character.

It was after a hectic six months of courtship that she'd met his younger brother, Grant. A year younger than Greg, he was almost his double. But he had one thing Greg lacked—character. At least Nina thought so. It was inevitable that she should give up Greg and fall in love with Grant.

And Grant reciprocated. He had been in Washington in an important minor post at the White House. Now he was back in his home state seeking the office of district attorney. He enlisted Nina's aid and she enthusiastically joined him in his campaign for office.

When they became engaged, Greg showed a good deal of resentment, but she hadn't paid much attention to it. At that time Republican Senator Thomas Ryan had begun to direct a lot of political pressure and opposition to Grant's candidacy. Ryan alleged that Grant Carter had underworld backing and that his personal life should be carefully investigated.

At a midnight supper in one of Boston's better restaurants Grant had sat across from her and explained that he was genuinely worried about what might happen.

"But all these things Senator Ryan has hinted about you are lies," she protested.

"I know that," Grant said with a troubled expression on his good-looking face. "But a lot of people are ready to believe him."

"You need a better campaign manager," Nina said.

"Mort Venn isn't so bad," Grant had insisted. Mort was a close friend of his college days who now owned a large advertising agency. Grant had naturally turned to him as campaign director.

Nina's impression of the big, prematurely-bald man wasn't all that favorable. "I think he's too easy-going," she said.

"He has an important advertising agency," Grant reminded her.

"Which he inherited from his father and which his employees run for him," she countered.

"I think Elise has a lot to offer," Grant said. Elise was Mort Venn's wife and had been an executive in the agency before she married Mort. She was blonde and lovely and still played a minor role in the business.

"Elise is smart and I like her," Nina had agreed. "Probably you ought to have her take a part in the campaign."

"I'll talk to her," Grant promised.

At the time Nina had not dreamed that she'd given Grant the worst advice possible. There were long intervals when she hardly saw him at all as the tempo of the campaign increased. Also, Grant's secretary, Kay Dunninger, did all she could to make it difficult for Nina to get in touch with him.

Nina learned later that the brunette Kay had long had a crush on Grant. She'd worked for him in Washington as a typical office wife and had come to Boston at his request. Kay had mistaken his appreciation of her talents as a secretary for an interest in her as a possible wife. When Kay learned that he was engaged to Nina, it had been a severe blow for her, but she'd continued as Grant's secretary.

The crisis came when the Boston *Globe* ran a story claiming that Grant Carter and the wife of his campaign manager, Elise Venn, were lovers and partners in a shady real estate deal in which land was sold to the state for a highway through information available only to Grant. To back up the charge the paper had published a series of typed letters Elise sent him along with Grant's replies signed with his initials. Grant tried to get in touch with Elise. But on the very afternoon the story appeared, she plunged from the narrow ledge of her apartment balcony to her death in the courtyard below. Her suicide was taken as an admission of guilt.

Mort Venn insisted that his wife had been drinking at the time and that her death had nothing to do with the scandal. The newspapers were extremely unkind to Grant in their coverage of the woman's death. There were witnesses who claimed they often saw Elise alone with Grant and although he stubbornly denied this, the scandal had all but ruined his campaign.

It was Nina who began to have suspicions that Grant was being made a scapegoat for someone else's wrongdoing. One day when she managed to see Grant in his office she told him what she'd come to believe.

"I think those witnesses have made a bad mistake," she said. "I think it was Greg they saw with Elise, not you."

"Greg?" he'd echoed in surprise. It had apparently not occurred to him that his brother might have been involved with the shapely blonde.

"Why not?" Nina had asked him. "Greg knew her well. All of you spent a good deal of time together. You say you didn't see Elise on the sly. Then it must have been Greg."

"You could be right," he agreed. "Greg is capable of that kind of thing and he always liked Elise. Maybe he was in on that land deal as well."

"You should find out," she said.

"With Elise dead it won't be easy," Grant warned her. "Greg is at Blue Gables on Pirate Island. I'll drive down there

16

tonight and ask him directly if he was involved with Elise!"

But Grant was destined never to reach Dark Harbor. It was on the drive there that he met with the accident that cost him his life. The tragedy had ended his campaign and the opposition's unfair attacks against him. But Nina made up her mind that Grant's name should be cleared and so she had accepted Greg's invitation to spend some time with the family at Blue Gables.

She believed that the invitation had been extended for more than mere kindness. She felt that Greg had an uneasy conscience about the affair with Elise and wanted to find out if she had any proof to link him with the dead girl. Having her at Blue Gables would offer an excellent opportunity to learn just how much she knew.

Since she was aware of this, Nina had accepted the invitation to Pirate Island with a good deal of uneasiness. But she was also filled with a purpose so she took Greg up on his offer.

Now she was installed as a guest in a large bedroom on the third floor overlooking the village of Dark Harbor and the ocean beyond. The other guests in the old mansion included the widowed Mort Venn and Grant's former secretary, Kay Dunninger. Greg had hired Kay to work for him and it was apparent that she'd transferred her loyalty for Grant to his older brother. Nina worried about this, as she'd hoped Kay would help to implicate Greg. This seemed unlikely now.

Also in the big mansion was Aunt Madge Carter, the only surviving member of her generation and the woman who had been responsible for raising Grant and Greg following their parents' death. She was an old woman now and shaken by Grant's death. But she still ruled the household and had a great deal of influence over Greg.

As Nina and Greg went down the several flights of stairs to

join the others, he said, "I'm afraid your vanishing as you did today could cause gossip."

"Why?"

"Everyone knows you and Grant were engaged. People might get the idea you have a guilty conscience."

"What about?" she asked with some annoyance.

He hedged. "Well, all that stuff in the newspapers. They might think you know more about it than you let on."

"You know that's not true," she said, aware that he was again trying to find out just how much she knew.

"And you weren't all that friendly toward me," Greg went on in an injured tone.

"I'm sorry," she said. "I try to be. It's only that you look so much like Grant that being with you makes me uneasy."

"That's a nice thing to tell me!"

"I'm afraid it's the truth," she said.

They reached the ground floor and went out onto the porch where the buffet had been set out. The others were already seated, eating from plates in their laps.

Aunt Madge Carter greeted Nina with an acid stare. She was a thin woman of medium height with dyed hair arranged so it looked like a wig. Her skin was flabby and she had an oval face with pale blue eyes which usually held a critical gleam.

The old woman said, "So you've decided to rejoin us!"

"Yes. I found the crowd at the party a little overwhelming," she said, going to the table and taking a plate to help herself to portions of the lobster, roast beef, turkey and other luscious offerings spread out on the gleaming white cloth.

At her side and filling his own plate, Greg said, "I think the party went very well. It was time we had one. Sort of takes some of the shadow from all of us."

The big, balding Mort Venn spoke from the easy chair in

which he was seated and said, "I'm afraid Grant's doings are still very much in the public mind. Quite a few people asked me about the various stories which have been spread about him."

Still at the buffet table Greg gave him a glance and said, "Didn't they know you were Elise's husband?"

"A lot of them didn't," the bald man said. "When they found out they got away from me fast!"

The dark, almost attractive Kay Dunninger raised her eyes from her plate to say, "People are such malicious gossips! You'd think they'd let the dead rest."

Greg went over to sit beside her, his plate heaped with food. "Not when the two dead people are as prominent and attractive as Grant and Elise were."

"Vicious talk!" Aunt Madge complained. "Let us not even discuss it secondhand." She turned to Nina, who had taken a chair beside her and asked, "Did you have a chance to talk with Mabel Renshaw?"

"You mean the actress?" Nina said. "No. I didn't know she was here."

"She came late. She's a striking woman," Aunt Madge said. "But she's about the only theatre person on the island now. Really important star, I mean. It was different in my youth. We had George Fawcett and his wife at Siasconset and they had DeWolfe Hopper and Louise Closser Hale and dozens of other stars here. The island was so much more interesting then."

"You've been saying that for years," Greg teased.

"And I mean it!" the old lady said indignantly. "Every year it becomes more of a tourist trap and less of a summer resort!"

Nina listened to this talk with mild interest. Grant had often chuckled about the arguments he and Greg had with their aunt. It seemed that the arguments were destined to go on. She finished her food and had some coffee. As she went back to her chair she noted that Greg and Kay Dunninger were having a rapt conversation.

She saw the admiring look on the dark-haired girl's long, almost horsey face and despaired of ever getting any important information against Greg from her. Kay was all too quick to transfer her affections to her current employer. Once hopelessly in love with Grant, Kay now appeared to be equally devoted to Greg.

When Nina finished her coffee she made an excuse to leave the porch and wandered out to the back garden. She was strolling out there when Mort Venn came out to her. He looked heavier than usual in his white sport jacket, dark shirt and tie and striped trousers.

"Do you mind if I join you?" he asked.

"No," she said. "I'm just enjoying the lovely night and the flowers."

"It is beautiful down here," Mort agreed. "I wasn't going to come. Then I decided a change would do me good."

"Are you feeling better?"

The bald man with the moon face and horn-rimmed glasses frowned. "Yes and no."

"Meaning?"

He gave her an uneasy glance. "I'm having some bad dreams again. Dreams about Elise."

"Oh!"

"I had them for a while after she killed herself," he went on. "Then they left me. But since I've been here, they've come back."

"Why?"

"I don't know," he said. "Maybe because she was with me here on my last visit."

20

"Did she come here often?" Nina asked.

"She was here quite a few times. You know she had an inquiring mind. She became interested in the history of the island."

"I had no idea she'd been a frequent visitor here."

"She was. Last night I dreamt about her again. She came and talked to me in the dream."

Nina stared at him as they stood in the growing twilight. "What did she say to you in your dream?"

"I can't remember," the big man said helplessly. "It was very mixed up."

"You ought to try. It might have some meaning."

"I doubt it," he said. "If I keep on having these dreams I think I'll go back to the mainland."

"Don't do that!" she protested. "That would ruin everything. I need you to help me!"

Mort stared at her suspiciously. "Need me for what?"

She hesitated. Then said, "Surely you know I've come here for a reason."

"A reason?" The none-too-bright Mort seemed baffled by her words.

Nina said, "I've never believed that story of Elise and Grant having an affair."

The big man looked unhappy. "I haven't wanted to. If it did happen, I guess it was something they couldn't help. Sometimes people just can't control their feelings."

"Grant was in love with me," she told him.

"I always was sure I was the only man for Elise," Mort Venn said. "She was the brains of the marriage. You know that I depended on her for everything."

"That's quite an admission."

"It's true," the big man said unhappily. "I've just been realizing that without Elise I'm nothing!"

"Don't you want to know the truth about what happened?"

A strange, grim look crossed the moon face. He said, "She killed herself. I guess she did it because she felt guilty and couldn't stand to go on making me unhappy."

"You believe her suicide was an admission that she loved Grant and was in a crooked partnership with him?"

"People don't kill themselves over minor things," he said.

"If you believe that, you are accepting the lies Senator Ryan tried to sell the public."

"Maybe they had truth in them," Mort said.

She gave him a sharp look of annoyance in the fading light. "Where were you when Elise killed herself?"

He showed surprise. "I was in the apartment with her. It was in all the papers. You must have read the account."

"I did," she said. "But I'd still like to hear it from you."

The big man frowned. "We'd had cocktails and were going out for dinner. She seemed her usual self, though now that I look back on it she did act kind of nervous. I went to my study to make a phone call. I was on the phone when I heard the crash and scream. I dropped the phone, went in and found the doors to the balcony open and when I looked down, I saw her sprawled on the asphalt of the courtyard."

"So you didn't actually see her take her life?"

"No. But I was right there."

Nina said, "Yet you don't know what impulse drove her to it."

"I guess not. When I left her she was finishing her drink. I suppose she was trying to find the courage to leap from the balcony."

"I wonder," Nina said.

"It's bad enough to have these dreams," he complained. "I don't want to go over all that happened that night again and again."

"I'm sorry," she said. "I'm only trying to get all the information I can about what happened. You hadn't accused her of being unfaithful with Grant. There had been no quarrel between you two."

"None," the big man said gravely. "Elise knew I didn't doubt her. I agreed that newspaper stuff was cooked up to ruin Grant's chances of being elected."

"So you had a perfect understanding?"

"I guess you could call it that," Mort said. "I trusted Elise and I knew Grant wouldn't play any dirty tricks on me."

Darkness had come to the garden while they discussed the dead woman. Nina went on, "But after Elise killed herself you changed your mind? You decided there had been an affair between them."

"I had to. She must have had a reason for taking her life. She hated herself for having deceived me."

"You're assuming that."

"I think it's the truth."

In a meaningful tone, she said, "Perhaps that is why you keep having those bad dreams."

The big man gaped. "I don't understand."

"You say in your dreams Elise is always trying to tell you something. Maybe her spirit is trying to get through to you and tell you the truth about her suicide."

"You think there was some other reason?"

"Yes."

Mort Venn seemed disturbed. "You're a strange girl," he said. "I think you ought to forget about Grant. He's dead. Nothing can change that. And Greg is in love with you."

"I don't happen to love Greg," she told him evenly. "And I do feel called on to clear Grant's name even though he's dead. That is why I'm here and why I'll need your help."

The big man said in a worried voice, "I think you're all

wrong, Nina. You should let the matter rest. But I'll do any-thing I can, just the same."

"Thank you," she said. "We'll have another talk about this later."

"If I decide to stay here. I don't like those dreams," the big man repeated.

"I want you to remain," she insisted. "I want everyone who is here to remain."

She left him and quietly made her way up to her room. Seated in a chair by the window she stared out at the lighted village below.

In the distance she could see the revolving beam of Gull's Point lighthouse. She thought over all that Mort had said and knew her task of proving Grant's innocence would not be easy. But she refused to think it hopeless.

She got up from her chair and moved to the other window which overlooked the gardens and lawns of the old mansion. And as she stared out into the moonlit garden she was surprised to see Mort Venn still there. He was standing in the pale blue moonlight gazing out toward the ocean. A little to his left Nina saw something which made her cry out.

Standing a few feet behind him and gazing at him with infinite sadness was the blonde ghost of Elise. There was no mistaking the flowing golden hair or the slim figure! Mort stood there quite unaware that the ghost of his wife was close enough to touch him on the shoulder!

Chapter Two

The eerie scene lasted only a moment. Then the phantom figure of Elise vanished as quickly as it had appeared and Mort Venn was left standing alone in the garden. As Nina watched with shocked fascination the big man slowly turned and gazed at almost the exact spot where the ghost of his wife had appeared. He seemed to see nothing for he then strolled back toward the house.

Nina withdrew from the window, her heart pounding. She tried to tell herself that it had been an illusion, something she'd imagined, but she knew this wasn't so. She'd recognized Elise's long blonde hair and the outline of her body. She'd already heard that Elise had been a frequent visitor at Blue Gables. Now she had come back to haunt it.

Mort's story of his weird dream had sent a cold chill down her spine. Having seen this vision on top of it left no doubt in her mind that the old mansion was haunted. And this made her think, "What if Grant's ghost returned, too?" Perhaps she'd stumbled onto something more frightening than she'd guessed.

She prepared for bed, her mind filled with troubled thoughts. And when she slept she had dreams of meeting Elise in the dark corridors of Blue Gables. Always the confrontation was frightening with the pale and lovely Elise having the transparent quality of a phantom. The ghost of the blonde girl moved slowly past her and did not look at her at

25

all. The dream kept repeating itself in different ways. Once Nina woke up perspiring with the bedclothes rumpled and pushed back.

She lay awake worrying for a long time before she was able to get some rest again. The next morning was sunny, typical island weather. The weird vision came back to her as she washed and dressed to go down and join the others.

Nina put on a yellow swim suit with a matching skirt over it. When she reached the breakfast table Aunt Madge Carter was seated there alone.

"Good morning," she said in her sharp way. "I trust you slept well."

"Except for a few dreams," Nina said, helping herself to orange juice from a plastic pitcher on the table. All the necessary ingredients for breakfast were within easy reach.

The pale blue eyes of the old woman fixed on her. "What sort of dreams?"

She hesitated. "Dreams about people."

"Most dreams are of people," Aunt Madge said with a testy shake of her head. "Can't you be a bit more precise?"

Nina felt a little annoyed at the old woman's impudent question and decided she would be quite candid in her reply. "Very well," she said. "I dreamt I saw Elise Venn. Elise as a ghost gliding down one of the corridors of this house."

She had not thought what reaction she might get to this from staid Aunt Madge and was not prepared for the one that followed. The old woman's white flabby face took on a frightened look and the pale blue eyes glanced nervously around to make sure they were alone before she leaned forward to ask, "Did you really dream that? You saw Elise's ghost?"

"Yes," she said, shocked at the old woman's behavior.

The thin lips of the mistress of Blue Gables trembled

nervously as she said in a low voice, "You may find it hard to believe but I'm certain I saw the ghost of Elise last night myself."

Nina stared at her. "You did?"

"I did," the old woman said. "I wouldn't have dared to mention it if you hadn't told me about your dreams just now. But under the circumstances I couldn't help telling you."

"That's very strange," Nina said, debating whether she ought to reveal that she also had seen the ghostly figure of the blonde woman in the garden.

"Yes," Aunt Madge Carter went on in a confidential tone, "I looked out my window. It was a moonlit night and the garden was beautiful. And there she was! I nearly stopped breathing."

The statement had somewhat the same effect on Nina. So the old woman had seen the ghostly figure in the garden just as she had! And she'd not even given her a clue by mentioning her own experience. It seemed to leave little doubt that the ghost of Elise had been roving the grounds in the night.

She said, "I wonder if Mort saw her?"

"I don't know," the old woman said, looking shaken. "He was at the table here for coffee but of course I couldn't mention it to him. He's out on the patio now with Greg reading the morning papers."

Nina recalled that when she'd seen Elise, the phantom had remained standing behind her husband, hiding from him. She said, "Perhaps she didn't want to appear before her husband."

"Perhaps not!" Aunt Madge agreed with a troubled look. "Imagine my believing in ghosts at my age. I have always been a strict skeptic until now."

"You have to believe what you've seen," Nina said as she poured herself some coffee.

27

"Please don't mention what I've told you to another soul!" the old woman pleaded.

"Of course not."

Aunt Madge looked unhappy. "Elise used to love it so here. She and Mort would spend a week at a time on the island. I suppose her ghost comes here because she is lonely in that other world."

Nina sipped her coffee and gave the old woman at the head of the table a knowing look. "Or perhaps she has something to say to Mort. Something she didn't have a chance to tell him before she took her life."

The pale blue eyes in the mottled face widened. "You think she may have a message for Mort?" she asked in an awed voice.

"I'd think it possible. The circumstances of her death are still a mystery. It was a tragedy and it somehow is linked with Grant's death in that they were both involved in that scandal."

Aunt Madge returned to her usual acid self. "I think it is wrong of you to bring that up—to probe into Grant's affairs after his death."

"I can't help myself. I loved him and I want to clear his name. There is no other way but to try and find answers to some of the questions his death raised."

The old woman protested. " 'Let the dead rest' is my motto! All that scandal about Grant and Elise is bound to evaporate now that they're both dead and no one is especially interested."

"I'm interested," Nina said firmly. "Grant and I were engaged. I know he was not mixed up with Elise as the papers made out."

"You should stop your spiteful probing," Aunt Madge warned her. "No wonder the ghost of Elise has shown herself.

28

It will be Grant's spectre we'll be seeing next!"

"I hope not," she said soberly, since she had worried about that same thing.

Aunt Madge touched a napkin to her thin blue lips. "And let me have your word that you won't mention what I have told you about seeing Elise."

"I promised you I wouldn't say anything. And I won't."

"And do relax and enjoy the island without delving into a tragic past that is better unexplored," the old woman begged her.

Nina shook her head. "I'm sorry, Miss Carter. That is something else again. I make no promises in that regard."

The old woman got up from the table in silence and, after giving her a last apprehensive glance, left the bright dining room. Nina sat there finishing her coffee and thinking of her strange conversation with the old woman. Through the partly open French doors she could hear the distant voices of Mort Venn and Greg Carter as they talked in low tones on the patio. She recognized the voices but could not clearly make out what they were saying.

When she got up from the table she went out to the stone patio which ran the length of the house and found Greg and Mort seated in wicker chairs, the papers at their feet. Both men were wearing bathing trunks and dark glasses as they relaxed in the bright sunshine. Mort's huge body was encased in vivid red trunks which accentuated his girth while Greg's slim black shorts made his lithe, bronzed body look even trimmer.

She paused for a moment, noticing that Mort's bald head was burning badly under the strong sun. "I'd watch that sun if I were you, Mort," she said.

The big man touched his head. "You're right! My skull feels like it's tingling all the way across. I'll be going in anyway. I plan to play golf this morning."

"Sounds like a lot of effort," Greg drawled. "I'm planning to take the boat out. Why don't you come along?"

"No," Mort said, still sprawled in the chair. "I promised Bettina I'd play her nine holes this morning and she'll he coming around for me in another quarter-hour."

The name was new to Nina. "Who is Bettina?" she asked.

Greg offered her a mocking smile. "Don't you know?"

"No."

"I thought everyone knew her," Greg said. "She bought the guest house here a few years ago. She lived in it with her daughter and son-in-law. He's a fairly famous artist and has a studio in the barn over there."

It was all news to her. She glanced across the lawn, beyond the swimming pool and the gardens and saw the neat Cape-style summer house and the large gray barn nearby. She'd never been over there. She said, "I'm sure I've never met them."

"They're interesting people," Mort Venn told her. "The mother has had a lot of experience in advertising. She worked for me when I was handling Grant's campaign."

"Oh!" Any mention of someone who'd in any way been connected with Grant and the campaign was of interest to her. Especially anyone she'd not previously met. Who could tell but some stranger might offer an all-important clue to proving Grant's innocence.

Mort gave her a warning glance. It seemed that he had read her thoughts. He said, "She wasn't all that close to Grant you know."

From his chair Greg gave a lazy laugh. "No, but Jeri was!"

"Jeri!" Nina said, stunned by this list of new names.

"Jeri is her daughter," Mort said, looking uncomfortable. "She is a lawyer. For a while she worked in Thomas Ryan's office but she isn't doing anything right now."

"Senator Ryan's office!" she exclaimed. "He's the one who made all those scandalous charges against Grant."

"That's right," Mort admitted. "But you can't blame Jeri for that. She just happened to work there."

"At the same time her mother was working in your office on Grant's campaign," she said unhappily, "Wouldn't that allow a lot of information to go back and forth?"

"I'm sure none did," Mort said lamely. "It just happened that way." He lifted his huge flabby body from the wicker chair. "Time I went inside and changed if I'm going to be ready for Bettina." And he lumbered off inside the house.

Nina stood in the lazy sunlight staring after Mort with a look of exasperation. She turned to the seated Greg and said, "Of course he left us because he didn't want to answer any more of my questions."

The handsome Greg smiled at her. "Can you blame him?"

"And you're on his side!" she accused him.

"I'm on the side of those who want to enjoy a sunny summer day and leave well enough alone," Greg said, staring at her from behind his dark glasses.

She sat in the chair which Mort had just vacated. "I can understand Mort's attitude," she said bitterly. "He's still upset by Elise's suicide and maybe not certain that she didn't have an affair with Grant. But I can't see why you are so casual about it all. Grant was your brother. You ought to want to clear his name."

Greg shrugged. "I told Grant before he tried for that political job that he should be sure his record was clean. He didn't pay any attention to me. I don't know how friendly he was with Elise or what they did concerning that fake land deal. Maybe they were guilty. They're both dead. It doesn't matter."

"I say it does," she retorted angrily. And she recalled that she and Grant had both suspected that it was Greg the dead girl had been seen with so frequently. If this were true it was understandable why Greg wanted the matter dismissed and forgotten.

Greg leaned forward and clasped his hands as he spoke earnestly, "Before you ever met Grant you were dating me. That ought never to have been broken up. You really didn't know Grant as well as you thought."

"I knew him well enough," she insisted.

"I wonder," Greg said with sarcasm. "He stole you from me very easily. And why not? He was used to that sort of thing. You may not want to accept it, but Grant was a womanizer. Even poor, plain Kay Dunninger was in love with him. She extols his virtues to me whenever she has a chance. And there were others. Girls you never met at all. So why be so sure he didn't have an affair with Elise?"

"You were jealous of Grant," she said. "That's why you say such things about him."

"Okay," Greg said. "I'll admit it. I hated him for stealing you among other things. Why shouldn't I have?"

"I'm sorry, Greg," she said. "We just don't communicate with each other. It's impossible for me to make you understand how I feel about Grant."

"I disagree. I think I know exactly how you feel and your feelings are all wrong," Grant's brother said. "I want to straighten you out so you'll forget him and come back to me again."

"That isn't apt to happen," she said.

"I can keep hoping," Greg said, standing. "In the meantime, why don't we enjoy a swim?"

"All right," she told him. They walked across to the kidney-shaped pool.

Greg went to the diving board, poised his supple body and dived expertly into the water with hardly any splash. She preferred to walk into the water gradually from the steps at her end of the pool.

His hair matted against his forehead, Greg appeared above the water and cried, "The water is just right."

"I know," she said. She was in it up to her waist as she answered and she then moved into the deeper water and swam out to join him.

He moved easily in the water. She thought he was probably a better swimmer than Grant had been. On the few visits she'd made to Blue Gables as Grant's fiancée she'd done little swimming. Grant had preferred to play tennis and drive around the island. He'd been especially interested in the old monastery which Derek Mills had mentioned.

As she swam at Greg's side, she told him, "I had a chat with Derek Mills yesterday."

"I didn't know you were friends," Greg said, sounding not too pleased.

"I'd hardly say we were friends. But Grant introduced me to him. I like him."

"One of the old island families," Greg said. "Too conservative for my taste. Though he did break out of his shell last summer. He had an affair with that Porter girl who was mixed up with the hippie colony. It was the talk of the island. You know his wife is a mental case in a mainland hospital."

She moved slowly in the water. "I don't think he'd do anything really wrong. He seems very nice."

Greg groaned. "There you go again! You refuse to believe anything bad about any attractive man. Except me, of course. I have to be the exception to the rule!"

She laughed at this and they went on swimming. All at once she was aware of someone on the diving board above them. And a moment later a third party joined them in the water. As she adjusted to the newcomer she saw that it was an attractive girl with a round face and a pert snub nose. The girl wore a white bathing cap but Nina was sure that she was dark-haired.

"Hello!" The girl said smiling and swimming happily up to them.

"Jeri!" Greg exclaimed with delight. "I missed you at the party yesterday."

"For the simple reason we didn't get there," Jeri said, keeping near them in the water. "Val and I took the ferry to the Cape and we didn't get back until early this morning."

"So that was it!" Greg said. And he turned to Nina and said, "I want you to meet Jeri! This is Nina, she was engaged to Grant just before he was killed."

Jeri gave her a friendly look. "Of course. He told me about you. I'm so sorry."

"Thank you," she said lamely not sure what to make of this Jeri whom she'd first heard about only a short while ago and who had now come abruptly into her life.

They swam about for a little longer with Greg livening up the fun by individually attacking each of the girls and trying to drag them under. They were still in the water when Nina saw Kay Dunninger in a proper white dress come striding across the lawn to the pool in her professional, secretarial manner.

The dark-haired girl stood by the poolside disapprovingly and said, "Your office wants you on long distance, Mr. Carter."

Greg's head bobbed out of the water and he groaned. "Can't you take the call, Kay?"

"I'm sorry, Mr. Carter, they asked expressly for you," the tall, thin girl continued in the same cold tone.

"All right, tell them I'll be right there," he said.

"Very well, sir," Kay said, and headed back to the old mansion.

Greg turned to the two girls in the pool. "That's the end of our fun! I should have a line run out to poolside so I could take my calls in the water. But Aunt Madge has always argued about it. I'll see you later." He moved to the edge of the pool, hauled himself up over the side and took a towel from one of the chairs. As he dried his dripping body, he smiled at them, "At any rate this will give you two a chance to get to know each other."

He left them and followed Kay Dunninger to the house. After a few minutes Jeri said that she'd had enough of the pool and Nina agreed. They both got out of the water and stretched out side by side on lounges to sun themselves.

Nina began their conversation by saying, "I can't imagine why we've never met before."

"It is strange," the other girl agreed. She had, as Nina had suspected, short black hair cut in the latest style.

"You worked with Senator Thomas Ryan?"

Jeri turned to smile at her. "I suppose you think that made me an enemy of Grant's?"

"It was the enemy camp."

"I had no part in the campaign," Jeri assured her. "I was busy looking after civil cases in the office. I wouldn't have been mixed up in that mud-slinging. Grant and I were too close for that."

"Really?" she commented in a small voice. She had never known about this girl until this morning and now she was hearing that the dark-haired beauty had been very close to Grant!

The snub-nosed Jeri offered her a teasing smile. "I know you won't hate me for it. But Grant and I were engaged for a time before he met you."

She was stunned. "He didn't mention it to me."

"Not likely he would have," Jeri said rather smugly. "You see I fell madly in love with Val Cramer, the artist, and ran off and married him. Grant never did forgive me for that."

Nina didn't know what to say. The thing that worried her most was that this was all new to her. Grant could have confided in her about this earlier engagement. And unhappily it began to appear that what Greg had said was true. Grant had been popular with a lot of young women she didn't know about.

She asked, "How long were you and Grant engaged?"

"Only a month or so," Jeri said, her eyes closed as she lazily soaked up the sun. "He never did get around to giving me a ring. But we were engaged."

"I don't suppose a ring is all that important," she said. The truth was that Grant had never gotten around to giving her one either. In fact Greg had taunted her about this.

"We've lived here on Pirate Island ever since my mother bought the summer house from Miss Carter," Jeri went on.

"So I understand."

"And now Val has his workshop and studio here in the summers," the pert-faced dark girl told her. "You must meet my husband. He's quite a remarkable fellow. He's a kind of sculptor," the girl went on as they lay there in the sun. "But he's rather different in his approach to it. He carves out of wood and uses other materials to make lifelike effigies."

"That does sound different," Nina agreed.

"You may have seen articles in the Sunday sections about him and his work," Jeri said. "He's based his art on a lost Scandinavian type of effigy-making. In ancient days in Norway and Sweden certain practitioners of witchcraft made these effigies to use in their rituals."

"I see," Nina said.

36

"It was a very special craft and only a few of those ancient effigies remain to be seen in museums," Jeri told her. "It seems the magic practitioners got themselves in bad repute. They made their effigies in likenesses of people they wished to harm or manipulate. And in the end people turned against them because of this, burned down their houses and destroyed the effigies. But a few were saved."

"Something like the voodoo practice of making clay models and sticking pins in them to make the people they resemble suffer and die," Nina said. She decided this was a singularly strange conversation and that Val Cramer must be an odd type of person.

Jeri raised herself on an elbow to tell her with an apologetic smile, "Of course Val would never indulge in any nonsense like witchcraft. But he does make effigies, life-size. Some of them are of famous people. He's been paid fabulous sums for a lot of them. They use them in advertisements, for displays and even as decorations in homes."

"You say they are carved from wood?"

"Just the heads and the body frames," Jeri said. "The rest he makes from other kinds of material."

"It sounds very interesting," she said.

The snub-nosed girl smiled wryly. "We're an interesting group. You've heard about mother?"

"Her name is Bettina?"

"Bettina Wells," her daughter promptly volunteered. "She's British you know. And she's fey!"

"Fey?"

"Clairvoyant," Jeri said in a tone which indicated she should have known the meaning of the word.

"Oh?"

"Yes. She can read palms. Tell you the most amazing things. And often her predictions come true! Not that I put too much stock in that. All fortune-tellers have the same trick, they tell you so many things some of them are bound to be right."

"I suppose so," Nina said faintly, somewhat overwhelmed by the dark girl's exuberance.

"And she has held spirit seances which have made my flesh creep," Jeri confided solemnly. "Not that I believe in them. But she has sat at a table with that crystal ball she uses and brought forth the most amazing messages. You'd swear she was talking with the dead."

This was becoming more and more amazing for Nina. She said, "But you don't believe any of it?"

Jeri's pert face shadowed. "No. If I did I'm sure I'd try and get her to have Grant talk to me." Then she looked embarrassed and quickly added, "Please don't misunderstand. I mean as a friend."

"I understand," she said, though she wasn't sure that she did or ever had.

Jeri sighed. "Poor Grant! What a bad time of it he had those last few months."

"I know."

The dark girl glanced at her with concern. "I'm sure that you did all you could to make him happy and that he was very much in love with you."

Nina smiled bitterly. "I felt that he was."

"But it was all those other things."

"I know."

Jeri, with the frankness she'd shown from their first meeting, asked her, "How did you feel about the newspaper stories that he was involved with Elise Venn?"

Nina stiffened. "I didn't believe it."

"Of course he would deny it."

"He said it wasn't true and I believed him."

"I'm not sure that Elise wasn't in love with him," Jeri went on. "I saw them together a lot. But I don't think Grant cared anything for her. And I don't think he was mixed up in that land deal with her."

"The evidence seems to prove otherwise," Nina said. "But I think that was manufactured."

"Mother has mentioned that," Jeri said. "You know she was working for Mort and Elise Venn's agency at the time the campaign was on."

"So I learned this morning."

"Only this morning?" Jeri's eyebrows raised.

"Yes, it's strange. This is all new to me."

The girl with the short dark hair said, "Of course Grant had told me about you. But I'd never met you."

"I see."

"I felt guilty working in Senator Ryan's office," Jeri went on in her glib fashion. "Especially when I suspected that the Senator's agents were producing a lot of false evidence against Grant."

"Did you tell Grant of your suspicions?" she asked the girl. She wondered if Jeri was as frank as she pretended to be or if all this exuberance might be a camouflage.

"I mentioned them to Mother when she was working on his campaign," Jeri said.

"But you weren't able to help him?"

"Not really. I was working in a different department of the law office. They kept me in the dark about those things. Perhaps because they found out I was a friend of Grant's." She added this last as if it were an afterthought, making Nina even more suspect of her than she had been.

"Things did close in on Grant just before his death," Nina agreed. "He was on his way here to have a private talk with Greg when he was killed."

"I know. What an awful way to die. And they never did find his body."

"There's a strong tide at that point," Nina said. "The police claimed his body was washed out to sea almost at once."

"I hope you're getting over it," the dark girl sympathized.

"In a sense. There are still things I'm anxious to find out," she said.

"Find out?" Jeri repeated, sounding bewildered.

"Yes," she said firmly. "I mean to keep questioning until I can prove that the charges against him were wrong."

Jeri's hazel eyes widened. "But Grant is dead!"

"What difference does that make?"

The dark girl hesitated, "I mean, who really cares anymore? Senator Ryan halted his campaign against Grant. The newspapers have dropped the story. With most people it's forgotten."

"Not with me," she said.

"I think I know what you mean," Jeri said, rather worriedly. "Though I'm not sure that you're wise."

Nina offered her a crooked smile. "Don't you think the reputations of the dead are as important as those of the living? Especially in the case of someone unfairly accused."

Jeri eyed her nervously. "But just suppose that the accusations against Grant were justified? Isn't it better to let the whole thing die."

"I have never believed him guilty," she said. "And I'm not afraid of what I'll find. Though I have reason to believe there are others who might be fearful."

A strange thing happened. The assured Jeri lost her poise and crimsoned. "Is that true?"

"I think so," she said.

Jeri quickly regained her easy manner and in her matter-of-fact way, she said, "Then I expect you'll have to go ahead with whatever it is you have in mind."

"Yes."

"Senator Ryan would be surprised if he knew that you mean to dig up all that old scandal," Jeri said.

"I doubt if he knows about me and my intentions," Nina said.

"Probably not," Jeri said. "I've lost touch with the office. After Grant's tragic death I didn't feel like working there any longer. I sort of felt he'd been hounded to his death."

Nina had the uneasy suspicion that the dark girl had said this chiefly for her benefit. But she pretended to take it at face value and agreed. "The scandal did force him to make that drive in a hurry. If he hadn't been on the road that night he wouldn't have been killed."

The dark-haired girl got up from the lounge and said, "I've had enough sun and pool. I'm going back to the house. But I'd like you to meet Val. Why don't you change and come across to the barn? He's at work there this morning."

Because Jeri had aroused Nina's interest in her husband and his art she wanted to meet him. Getting up with the other girl, she said, "All right. I'll be about a half-hour."

"I'll be there by then," the dark girl promised. "Come straight in. His workshop is at the rear of the barn and we'll probably be in there."

Nina thanked her again for the invitation and went back to the house. She had a quick shower in her room and changed to a white pants suit for the excursion to the barn. When she came downstairs she passed the study door and heard Greg dictating a letter to Kay Dunninger. Not wishing to disturb them she continued on and out of the old house.

She marched straight across the lawn still debating her opinion of Jeri Cramer. She wasn't sure whether the young lawyer was a friend or foe. The girl could be friendly and yet not reveal much about her true feelings, she decided.

Within a few minutes she reached the entrance to the workshop. The door and window trim of the gray, weathered barn had been painted bright red. A red sign with yellow lettering above the door, announced, "Cramer Gallery, Unusual Sculptures." Following Jeri's advice she opened the door and went straight in. She found herself in a gloomy reception area walled with black fabric. As she closed the door behind her the gloom increased. She took a few steps down the corridor and then halted with a cry of fear. For there, staring at her from a dark alcove in the wall, was a ghostly figure with long flowing blonde hair—the ghostly figure of Elise.

Chapter Three

It took Nina a moment to recover from the shock of seeing the figure in the shadowed nook. At once she realized that it wasn't the ghostly apparition she was seeing again but an effigy of Elise. The sculpture was truly a work of art and suspended from the black curtained wall it seemed alive. The face was a good likeness, but on close inspection it was evident that it was carved from wood.

Yet the hair seemed human and the eyes had a real look which made Nina wonder if glass had not been inserted in the wooden skull. Even the clothing was similar to what Elise had worn.

Nina heard a footstep from down the corridor and a fully dressed Jeri appeared. The dark girl was wearing shorts and a green sweater. She smiled and asked, "Did the effigy of Elise frighten you?"

"I wasn't expecting it," she admitted, not ready to tell this new acquaintance that only last night she'd seen the ghostly form of Elise in the garden of Blue Gables.

Jeri stood and admired the figure. "Val did it some time before Elise killed herself. She came here and modeled for him several times. The rest he did from photographs. I think it's a fine likeness."

"I agree," Nina said, somewhat tensely. "Did Elise ever see it?"

"Just once," Jeri said. "About six weeks before she jumped

from that balcony. She said it made her uneasy. It made her think of a corpse. Of course, I don't agree."

Nina shuddered. "I imagine it would give one a shock to see oneself in effigy like that."

"Perhaps," Jeri said casually. "At any rate it wasn't long before she was a corpse. I sometimes wonder if she didn't have a flash of ESP and ignored it."

"Strange," she agreed.

"Come on down the corridor," Jeri said leading the way. "On the right there is another figure. An old resident of the island named Captain Zachary Miller. His father and grandfather sailed the seven seas in clipper ships built in New England. And he was the skipper of an ironclad freighter in his day. He knew Joseph Conrad. He's over eighty now and lives in his own house in Dark Harbor."

Nina paused before the figure of the old captain and found it even more lifelike than the figure of Elise. The wizened face of Captain Miller showed a great deal of character and his clothing was typical of a retired mariner.

She said, "That's very interesting."

"Val had them set out in these alcoves to give a vivid impression. I'm not sure it conveys the feeling he wanted. I think it may even frighten people a little."

Nina said, "The effect is that of a museum if that is what your husband wished."

"I think it is," Jeri said. They had reached the end of the corridor and she opened the door into a large bright room with several workbenches filled with every sort of woodworking equipment. The walls were hung with completed effigies, and there were figures in various stages of completion stacked on the benches and tables. The floor was heaped with shavings and the room had the odor of freshly cut wood.

From an open doorway at the right of the room a tall, rangy

man with a Lincolnesque beard appeared. He was thin and tanned and had a rather loose-limbed, ungainly appearance. His large hook nose and the beard gave him an amazing likeness to the Civil War President. Yet there was none of Lincoln's kindliness in his lined face nor in his hard, rather smallish eyes.

"This is Val Cramer, my husband," Jeri said with some pride. "Val, I want you to meet Nina Patton, she's the girl who was engaged to Grant at the time of his death."

Val offered her a huge hand. She shook hands with him feeling terribly short. She was sure he must be over six feet tall.

She said, "I'm impressed by your work."

The small eyes studied her with interest. "Are these the first effigies of this sort you've seen?"

"Yes. They are not all that common," Nina said.

He smiled with obvious satisfaction. "I'm the only one in New England making them. Perhaps the only one in the United States. The craft went out of fashion because in the old days the masters of the trade were regarded as dealing in witchcraft."

"So I've heard," she said.

Val Cramer waved at the effigies hanging on the wall. "I've been able to give the craft a good reputation and I've had many noted people allow me to sculpt them."

Jeri said, "He did a magnificent one of Marilyn Monroe. A Hollywood director bought it shortly after her death."

Nina said, "And she was apparently a suicide like Elise. Do you only tend to do people who end up as suicides, Mr. Cramer?"

The man with the Lincoln beard smiled coldly. "That's the sort of supposition that made people believe effigy masters dealt in witchcraft in the old days."

"I'm sorry," she apologized. "I didn't mean it that way. I

was merely struck by the coincidence."

"That was quite natural," Jeri said quickly, defending Nina against her grim-faced husband.

Val Cramer relaxed and said, "I'm not upset by your comment. I only pointed out what talk of that sort could and did lead to in a more superstitious era."

Jeri grimaced. "Was there ever a more superstitious era than our own? More people believe in ghosts and Satanism than ever before. And you've heard Mother give her palm readings to awed friends."

The tall bearded man said with a disgusted tone, "Let's not use your mother as an example, Jeri. She's a rather special case."

Jeri turned to Nina and said, "I suppose I needn't tell you that my mother and Val don't get along too well."

"That isn't so unusual either," Nina said with a smile.

"I agree, Miss Patton," the artist said. "You can see the kind of labor that is required to put my effigies together from the ones in production here."

"It is impressive," Nina said.

"In the room from which I just came I have a display of completed figures," he said. "Jeri can take you in there and show you around while I go back to work." As he finished speaking he went to a bench and sat down with a life size head of wood on which he was apparently carving a face.

"I hope I'm not interrupting you," Nina apologized.

He glanced up from his carving. "Not at all. Jeri can take over."

Jeri led the way to the door opening in the display room. She said, "A lot of the figures have been sold recently. We haven't more than two dozen here now."

Nina followed her into the room and saw that again the walls were draped in black cloth and the effigies attached to the cloth so that they seemed to stand alone. It gave them a startling, life-like appearance. The effigies were set out along the walls all around the room. There was no special lighting other than the sunlight which streamed in from two windows rather high on one wall.

She studied the figures one after another and felt that she was in a kind of waxwork museum. The figures were grotesque in their reality. She came to one that obviously represented Judy Garland in her later years. The worn face and large haunted eyes were frighteningly real.

"Was it done before her death?" she asked.

"Yes," Jeri said. "I think almost a year before."

Nina moved on past other men and women whose likeness in this weird artform meant nothing to her. And then she halted before one with a chill racing down her spine and a look of grim amazement on her pretty face. It was an effigy of Grant Carter, the man to whom she'd been engaged.

Jeri noticed her reaction and apologized, "I should have warned you."

"It's Grant!" she said in a tense voice. And then as an afterthought, "Or perhaps your husband meant it to be Greg?"

"It's meant to be Grant," Jeri said. "Although they do look so much alike it could be Greg."

"When was it done?" she asked.

Jeri said, "About the same time he did Elise. As I recall, they both came over here to pose for the carvings."

"Oh?" she said. This was evidence that the two had come to the island together. Did it indicate something more?

"Grant saw the completed effigy and liked it better than Elise did hers. But then Grant was not at all superstitious," Jeri said.

"No, he wasn't," she agreed.

They went around and viewed the remaining figures, but this was an anticlimax after the shock she'd received from seeing Grant among the effigies. When they'd completed the tour they went back out to the workroom.

From his bench Val Cramer glanced up at her. "You've had the full tour," he said.

"Yes, thank you," she said. "You're doing very exciting work."

The tall young man smiled in his rather secretive way. "I think it is different."

"Thank you again," Nina said. "I won't stay to hold you back from your work."

She and Jeri went back along the corridor past the effigies of Captain Zachary Miller and Elise Venn. Then they emerged in the open sunlight again and Nina felt a distinct air of relief. There had been something sinister about the barn and the artist and his effigies.

The dark-haired Jeri was giving her an interested look. "How did you like them?"

"Terribly exciting," Nina said.

"He does well with them," Jeri agreed. "You have no idea how hard it is to get a likeness as well as he does."

"I'm sure it takes great talent," she said.

Jeri smiled. "I must ask him to do you."

Nina found herself almost in a panic as she quickly said, "No, please don't!"

The dark girl looked surprised. "Why not?"

Nina fumbled for words and finally came up with, "I think he ought to be left alone to select his own subjects. I wouldn't want him to do me because either you or I asked him."

"If he does you it will be his own idea," Jeri assured her. "And I somehow have an idea he may decide you'd make a suitable subject."

"Please don't try to influence him!" Nina begged her.

"I won't," Jeri said. "I'm glad you came over. We must see more of each other."

"Yes, I hope so," she agreed nervously.

They said goodbye and Jeri went back into the barn studio while Nina started back to the main house. The visit to the studio had been an experience she'd not soon forget. What nagged at her was the number of subjects Val had sculpted who had come to violent ends. And now he was proposing to do her, or at least his wife had hinted that he was.

Nina had no desire to be sculpted in effigy by Val Cramer. In retrospect she felt it was because of the way she'd first stumbled upon the likeness of Elise in that dark corridor. It had given her a shock from which she'd not recovered. And then seeing Grant a little later had been almost equally unpleasant. She did not consider herself superstitious but she was left with the feeling there was something not quite right about Val Cramer and his studio of effigies.

By the time she reached Blue Gables, Mort Venn had returned from his golf game and was entertaining a middle-aged woman on the patio. Nina had no choice but to speak to them on her way to the house.

Mort Venn in dark slacks and gray sweater looked less overweight than he had in a bathing suit. The eyes behind his horn-rimmed glasses showed good humor as he stood to greet Nina.

"I cut my handicap by twelve this morning," he informed her. "And I won the match from Bettina."

"Congratulations," she smiled. And she turned to the woman seated in the wicker chair. Bettina Wells in no way resembled her daughter. She was a hearty British type with strong, somewhat mannish features relieved by twinkling blue eyes and a head of long golden hair. The hair had to be a dye job but it was a skillful one.

Mort Venn introduced them and said, "I told you that Bettina worked on Grant's campaign."

The British woman winced visibly and said, "Please, I can't take any credit for that."

Nina told her, "I'm sure you did your best." She was sizing up the woman and trying to decide who she liked best, mother or daughter. And she decided it was impossible to tell since neither of them were fully revealing themselves. It was as if they were both playing carefully rehearsed roles. At least that was the feeling they gave her.

Mort Venn's round face showed gloom as he said, "It was a dirty campaign Senator Thomas Ryan waged and our agency wasn't the sort to deal with it."

Bettina Wells gave him a sharp glance. "I think Elise might have managed. But after her death it was all downhill."

Nina said, "I met your daughter for the first time this morning, Mrs. Wells. She's very nice and she told me she worked for Senator Ryan at the time of the election."

The golden-haired woman frowned. "Jeri was in Ryan's law office, but she had nothing to do with the campaign."

"She made that clear to me," Nina said.

"It was a strange situation," Bettina Wells said. She gave Nina a hesitant glance. "Especially as Jeri and Grant Carter were very close at one time."

She nodded. "She told me that this morning. They were engaged."

"Yes," Bettina said. "I wondered if you knew. Not many people were told."

"I didn't until Jeri told me," she said.

"Well, it was all very sad," Bettina Wells said. "I can't think what could have made poor Elise take her life. And as if that wasn't bad enough, Grant had to die in that accident."

"It was a strange sequence of events," Nina agreed. "At least it ended the election feud."

"No doubt of that," Morton Venn agreed and took a drink from his glass.

Bettina gave her a questioning look. "Did you meet my son-in-law?"

"The artist? Yes. Jeri took me to his studio," she said.

"Remarkable talent, hasn't he?"

"Without a doubt," Nina agreed.

The woman in the chair suddenly looked grim. "Though I must say I wish he wouldn't waste it on those effigies. They're a sick-looking lot as far as I'm concerned. That workshop of his reminds me of a charnel house."

Nina smiled faintly. "I'd hardly say it was that bad."

Mort Venn spoke up, "His specialty has made him nationally known. If he were doing ordinary sculpture or art he might not be noticed."

"I'd prefer that," Bettina Wells declared. "I don't like what he is doing. It gives me the creeps."

"The figures do give one a strange feeling," Nina agreed. "But then so do the figures in a waxworks if they are well-done."

"I have a feeling for the psychic," the woman in the wicker chair said. "And I get goose pimples every time I go in that place. Especially when I look at the effigies of the dead he has there. It's like a crypt, if you ask me."

Mort Venn chuckled. "I must take you there before we have our next game of golf. Then I'll be sure to beat you!"

"You would too. Not that you didn't manage well enough today," Bettina Wells said. She rose from the chair. "I must go home." She smiled for Nina's benefit. "It has been nice meeting you."

"And I've enjoyed meeting you," Nina said. "I'd like to

have another talk with you some time and hear more about the campaign."

"There's not all that much to tell," Bettina Wells said, looking suddenly ill at ease. "But we will have another talk."

The stout Mort Venn saw the British woman on her way and then came back to join Nina on the patio. He said, "What do you think of her?"

"She's interesting."

"I think so," Mort said. "I wish she'd come back and work for the agency but she seems to have lost interest."

"I wonder why?"

"I think she doesn't have to work. She has money of her own."

"That must be it," she said. "I don't suppose Val Cramer makes too much for his effigies and her daughter has given up her law career for a time at least. They must have enough to live on."

"I'm sure they do," Mort said. "Cramer comes from a wealthy family. I have an idea they give him a yearly allowance."

She smiled ruefully. "I'm getting a picture of how the other half lives."

"There are a lot of wealthy people here on Pirate Island and especially in the Dark Harbor area. The Carters certainly can't be termed poor."

"That is true," she agreed.

"What did you think of Cramer's studio?" the big man asked her.

She grimaced. "I ran directly into a likeness of Elise and then one of Grant. I was upset by them."

"You shouldn't have been. They were done long before either of them died."

"I still found it a strange experience," she said. "Perhaps I'm too sensitive."

She went inside and up to her third-floor bedroom to freshen up for luncheon. The morning had brought some odd experiences. Until a few hours ago she had not known of the existence of Jeri and Val Cramer or Bettina Wells. Yet all three were living on the Carter estate and all three had known both Grant and Elise.

It meant that she had three other people to consider and question in her attempt to establish the innocence of Grant. She wasn't sure that any of them would be of much help but she could at least try to get information from them. There was a strangeness about the trio which she could not readily put her finger on. And she had not felt truly at ease with any of them.

When she went downstairs, the others were all gathered at the luncheon table. Aunt Madge presided in her usual sharp way, Greg, for once, taking second place. It seemed that his domineering aunt was the only one who could make him behave quietly.

He announced, "I have to go to the mainland overnight. Are there any errands I can do for anyone?"

Aunt Madge spoke up, "You can stop by the Ritz Carlton and get me a copy of *Boston Magazine* from the newsstand. I didn't get my copy this month."

"Very well, Aunt Madge," the young man said. "Any other requests?"

There were none. The conversation continued and there was a long discussion about the adequacy of the ferry service from Woods Hole on the Cape. Mort Venn thought there should be late-night service for those who wished to spend the evening in Boston.

Greg Carter dismissed the idea with, "It wouldn't work, Mort. There wouldn't be enough traffic and a night ferry could be very dangerous. We have bad fogs and high winds at times."

"I'm only a visitor," the big man acknowledged, admitting he was no authority on the matter.

Kay Dunninger said very little though she listened to everything that Greg said with rapt attention, her expression often showing approval of his remarks. Nina recalled Kay had behaved much like this when she had been Grant's secretary. It seemed the girl needed a hero figure to worship and she proceeded to find one in her various employers.

After the meal was over Nina made it a point to leave the room with Greg's secretary. She wanted to question Kay a good deal more about the events leading up to the campaign and the ensuing scandal.

As they stood together in the hall, Nina told the girl. "I want you to think about all the things Grant discussed with you during his campaign for district attorney."

The girl looked surprised. "Why?"

Nina said, "You must realize that my reason for being here is to try and learn the truth about those days. I want to clear Grant's name and also see that Elise is no longer a subject for gossip. I'm positive there never was an affair between them as the press said."

Kay looked unhappy. "I'm not sure that anything I remember will be of value to you, Miss Patton."

"Call me Nina," she said. "I know you admired Grant."

"I did!"

"Then you should be willing to do anything you can to help," she said.

"I would like to help," Kay assured her. Then she looked worried. "But what does Mr. Greg think about it?"

She sighed. "Greg is not enthusiastic but I'm sure he won't be angry with you if you help me."

"As long as he doesn't object," Kay said. "He is my boss now. I can't very well cross him."

"I'll take any blame," Nina said. "And I have an idea Greg will be delighted if I can prove the scandal about his brother and Elise was a put-up job." She didn't add that there was a possibility Greg had a role in the scandal since she knew this would only frighten Kay. And in any case she wasn't sure yet that Greg bore any guilt.

Kay said, "What do you want me to try to remember?"

"Think of the various times you saw Elise and Grant together," she said. "And try to remember as much of their conversations as you can. That will do for a start. Later you can tell me if any of the things they said had any link with the story of their affair and the land deal."

The secretary's long face showed anger. "I never did believe those things about Grant and Elise Venn," she said.

Nina offered her a weary smile. "Nor did I. Now we must try to prove what we believe. And I'm counting on you to help."

"I'll try."

"That's all I ask," Nina said.

The girl went to the study, where Greg had set up a kind of office, and Nina walked out a side door to the patio. She was all at once filled with a desire to get away from the old mansion. So she went out back, got into her small foreign car and drove away.

She drove without any particular destination. The car was a convertible and she had the top down to enjoy the salt air and the sun. First she headed down to the village of Dark Harbor. She drove down its cobblestoned main street which slanted sharply toward the wharf. It was at this wharf that whaling ships had docked in the great days of the island.

Then the harbor had been a vast sea of masts. And the very cobblestones over which she now drove had come to the island as ballast on the many trading vessels which called there. In those days it was said the main street had been lined with taverns and legend had it that on dark, foggy nights when all the island was asleep the ghostly voices of those long-dead sailors and the music from the taverns could be heard.

When she reached the wharf area, she swung the little car around and drove up the street. This time she noted the Gray Heron Hotel and adjoining bar, owned and operated by Matthew Kimble, a dour man whose grandfather had suddenly appeared in the village one stormy night. He had at once let it be known he had unlimited funds to buy property and proceeded to do exactly that. Yet none of the islanders trusted him, many whispered he was in league with the Devil himself, while others suggested he was hiding out on Pirate Island after having made a fortune in the slave trade. Black ivory had been the basis of many a fortune.

Now the third generation of Kimbles was operating the inn, but the family was still not popular on the island. And Matthew Kimble had been in a mainland prison for some unknown crime. All that was known was that he'd spent several years in prison. Then he'd returned as dour and uncommunicative as ever. There were few who dared to cross the innkeeper in any way.

These stories about the island Nina had heard from Grant when they were first engaged and he'd brought her to this quaint spot where he'd spent so much of his youth. The memory of those happy times caused the familiar pain to rack her. And she bleakly wondered if she would ever get over losing Grant.

Certainly Greg had not been much help, nor had he shown any tenderness. The faults she'd first discovered in Greg were still very apparent. He was conceited and selfish. He'd made a halfhearted attempt to be pleasant at times, but all too often his displays of affection ended in anger.

For this she blamed herself as well as him. She knew that she left much of herself behind with the dead Grant. And it would stay with him until she uncovered the scandalous plot which had darkened his last days. Even then she might not be free. Others had loved Grant and gotten over it. Why should she be the exception? Perhaps because her love had more depth than that of a Jeri.

As these thoughts ran through her mind she drove away from the village and across the island in the direction of the museum. She did it almost unconsciously. And not until she drew up before the imposing building did she realize that she'd wanted to talk to Derek Mills. She parked the car and went in to ask for the young man she had come to like so much.

The receptionist sent her upstairs to his office. She passed through the main display room of the big museum and saw that an exhibit of model ships was being featured. There was also an art display of fine sailing ships and a collection of marine relics pertaining to the history of the island.

At the top of the stairway she entered a small office where Derek Mills' personal secretary sat. The girl smiled at her and asked. "Is there anything I can do for you?"

"Is Mr. Mills in?" she asked. "I'd like to speak with him."

"I'm sorry," the girl said. "He's out."

"Will he be back soon?"

"Not until later this afternoon," the girl said. "And I'm really not positive about that. It would be best to plan to see him tomorrow. He'll be here at the museum all day."

"Thank you," Nina said. "That's what I'll do." She was about to leave when she saw a familiar figure emerge from Derek Mills' private office. It was the ancient sea captain, Zachary Miller, whose effigy she'd seen in Val Cramer's studio.

The old man told the receptionist, "I've got the records on

those three-masted schooners corrected for Mr. Mills. You can tell him the notes are all on his desk."

"Fine," the pleasant girl said. "I'll tell him as soon as he comes in."

Captain Miller prepared to leave as Nina, who had hesitated on seeing him, smiled and said, "This is the second time I've seen you today, Captain Miller."

The old man looked surprised. "Is that so?"

"Yes," she said. "The first time was when I saw you in effigy at Val Cramer's Studio."

The old man moved across the office and nodded. "Yes. I know about that. He's a young man of considerable talents. Not that I think he ought to waste them making replicas of me."

Nina laughed. "I'd say you were a most interesting subject."

"Thanks," the Captain said dryly as they strolled out of the office and headed for the stairs together. "Seeing myself like that gave me a start at first, but I've been there a few times and now I'm used to it."

"I recognized you at once."

"I'm Zachary Miller," the old man said doffing his peaked cap.

"Glad to meet you Captain," she said. "I'm a house guest at the Carters. I was once engaged to Grant. My name is Nina Patton."

The bronzed, wizened face showed sympathy. "I knew young Grant. He was my favorite. Too bad about him."

"Yes, it was," she agreed as they descended the stairs together.

"Couldn't understand why they didn't try harder to locate his body," Captain Miller said.

"Because of the tide."

"I know the tide is bad there," the old Captain said. "But if they had started at once and made a real effort they should have been able to locate the body."

"It was too bad," she agreed.

They reached the ground floor and he showed her around the various displays, explaining the differences in the ships and giving her the histories of the various models. It developed that he had constructed some of them himself.

Captain Miller pointed out the model of the *Essex* whose side was stove in by a whale and whose crew spent ninety-three days in open boats before the survivors were rescued. This had happened in 1820.

"Extreme suffering," the old captain told her. "Cannibalism and all the rest of it! Out of twenty men aboard only eight survived."

When they left the museum she offered to drop the old man off at his house and he gladly accepted her offer. He explained that he had an ancient car which he sometimes drove but that it was being overhauled at the moment. He directed her toward the central part of Dark Harbor and then had her turn down a narrow sidestreet. His cottage was near the end of the street.

He got out of the car and after thanking her, said, "Any time you happen to be along this way I'd be glad to have you drop by for a cup of tea or a taste of rum." He smiled as he gave her the invitation.

"Thank you," she said. "I'd like to come by some day and perhaps you could tell me some stories about Grant when he was a boy here."

Captain Zachary Miller nodded. "I saw a lot of him in those days." He gave a deep sigh. "I sure wish they had found his body after that accident."

"I know," she said. "It bothered me, too."

The old man frowned. "I can't think of him resting with his body washed out to sea like that. Some of the islanders have a belief about bodies that aren't found."

"Oh?"

"Yes," Captain Miller said, fixing a rheumy eye on her. "They claim that the souls of those drowned whose bodies are lost can't rest. They keep coming back to the places they knew in life. If that's the case I'd reckon Grant's ghost would be bound to find its way back here."

Chapter Four

The old Captain's haunting story left Nina badly depressed as she drove back to Blue Gables. Strangely, it had not been the ghost of Grant who'd been stalking her nights but that of Elise! It could be that the ghost of Grant would yet appear and while she couldn't picture herself being afraid of his spirit, she did not know just how she would feel.

Her next reaction was to scoff at the whole idea. Before all these tragedies had happened she would have given scant attention to such ghost stories. But the grim patter of events had left their mark on her. She had no doubt that she had seen Elise's phantom figure, and now she listened to every ghostly yarn with a degree of credulity.

She drove into the rear driveway of Blue Gables and left her car. Mort Venn was sitting on the patio dressed for dinner. He wore a white linen suit and stared moodily into space as she joined him.

Nina paused and said, "Would your thoughts be worth a penny?"

"It would be a bad bargain," Mort said grimly.

"Did Greg leave for the mainland?"

"Yes. He said not to expect him until the morning."

"What about Kay?"

"She didn't go," Mort Venn said. "I don't think the trip had anything to do with his regular business. It was some private thing."

"I see," she said. "I drove around for a while. I find myself restless."

"I know," the advertising executive said.

She knew she had a little while before she had to change for the evening meal and so she sat down in one of the wicker chairs. Staring at the flagstone floor of the patio she said, "I met an old Captain. We had a chat. And he told me a creepy story about people who drown whose bodies aren't found. He claims their ghosts keep coming back to their old haunts, that they can't rest in the spirit world."

Eyebrows raised, Mort said, "A nice cheery yarn!"

"I know," she said. "I must say it upset me."

"It would."

She frowned. "I felt they didn't try hard enough to locate Grant's body."

"You don't believe that ridiculous story about the ghost coming back, surely?"

"No," she said reluctantly. "But after a while you begin to believe almost anything."

"I know," the stout man said.

She gave him an even look. "What would you say if I told you that I had seen the ghost of your wife here?"

Mort registered shock. "Elise?"

"Yes."

"I'd say you were imagining things."

"You'd be wrong."

"What?" The stout man leaned forward in his chair, staring at her as if she'd suddenly lost her mind.

"I'm positive I did see her and someone else here told me they had seen her, too."

Mort Venn's round face was a picture of dismay and behind the horn-rimmed glasses, his eyes narrowed anxiously. He said, "You're talking sick. Nina, I don't like it!"

"I think you're entitled to the truth."

"Go on."

"The other night you took a late stroll out here on the lawn."

"Yes."

"I went to the window and saw you."

"And?"

"And while I was watching a ghostly figure came up from behind and studied you sadly. It was Elise."

Mort sank back in his chair. "I saw no one."

"No. She vanished before you turned around. But I saw her. I recognized her long blonde hair."

The stout man was clearly stunned by what she'd told him. He said, "I don't know what to say."

"I don't care what you say," she told him calmly. "That is what I saw."

Mort Venn shook his head. "Maybe you ought to see a doctor, Nina. Some good psychiatrist. You've been brooding on Grant's death too long."

"This has nothing to do with that."

"I think it has," he said. "Greg is worried about you, too. He says you're all wrong in trying to get to the bottom of those stories about Grant and Elise. He thinks you're only going to cause trouble."

"I know his opinion and I'm not impressed," she said.

"You should be," the big man said. "Greg is in love with you. He'd marry you in a minute if you'd say the word."

"I don't love him."

"Why not? He and Grant looked enough alike to be twins!"

"I'm not thinking of appearances," she said. "There's a vast difference between them as men. Grant was much more sincere and considerate."

"I wonder," Mort said, giving her a knowing glance.

She said, "You're thinking about the stories they told. You

surely don't believe that he was unfaithful to me. That Elise and he were lovers?"

"Elise killed herself."

"I think none of us knows the true reason for that."

"The papers said it was because she was in love with Grant and they'd been caught in that crooked land deal," Mort said.

"You're ready to believe that?" Nina demanded. "If Elise and Grant did so well on that crooked land deal, what happened to the money from it? That's one of the questions I want to find out. We didn't locate any of it in Grant's accounts nor in Elise's."

Mort said, "There must have been a secret account which no one has found."

"I don't think so."

"What then?"

"I don't think they ever received that money. Someone else put through the deal and forged those papers to make it seem it was them. Perhaps Senator Ryan himself had something to do with it."

"I wouldn't know about that."

Nina said, "I think that Jeri Cramer should be able to find out."

"She doesn't work for Ryan any longer."

"No. But she surely must have some contacts in the office. I intend to ask her about that." She gave Mort a sharp look. "I never knew about her existence or her mother's until today. Why didn't you ever mention them?"

"They didn't seem important to me."

"Everyone who knew Elise or Grant can be important," Nina told him.

Mort said, "I wonder why Grant didn't mention that girl to you if he was so sincere. Why he didn't tell you he'd once been engaged to her."

64

"I don't know," she said, realizing that Mort had made a strong point. It bothered her that Grant had never mentioned Jeri. Still he might have had a perfectly good reason for not doing so. He might simply have forgotten her. There had been plenty of other things on his mind in the last months of his life.

Mort Venn pointed a stubby forefinger at her. "Maybe Grant led a whole secret life you don't know anything about."

She'd thought of this. "I doubt it. Do you think the same might be true of Elise? Do you think your wife might have been in love with Grant all that long while and you didn't guess?"

"I trusted Elise," Mort said heavily. "I didn't pry into every minute of her time."

"I think you were right to trust her. When the scandal broke you must have had some straight talk with her. Didn't you question her?"

"Yes."

"What did she say?"

"Nothing."

"I can't believe that."

Mort said, "She told me I ought to believe her and ignore what the papers said. And I did."

"And then?"

"We're in the apartment together and suddenly she throws herself from the balcony. After that I began to feel she'd been guilty and couldn't face it."

"But she'd been drinking, hadn't she?"

"Yes," said the big man in the white linen suit. "The papers had been unusually cruel that day and she began drinking after she read them."

Nina felt she was getting closer to this incident than she'd ever been before. Looking directly at Mort she suggested, "Would you say that she'd had a lot to drink? In other words, that she was drunk?"

He appeared reluctant to answer. Then he said, "She might have been."

"I read the account of the coroner's inquest," Nina told him. "According to the inquest she had a high level of alcohol in her blood."

Mort scowled. "So maybe she was drunk."

"Drunk and badly upset," Nina pointed out. "So isn't it possible that she stumbled and fell from that balcony by accident?"

"Yes, I suppose so."

"And if that is what happened there need be no question of guilt as a motivation."

"That's right," he agreed.

Nina felt a small triumph. "So your assuming that she took her own life because she was guilty of an affair with Grant is really negative thinking."

"If you put it like that."

"Isn't that what you'd prefer to think?"

He sighed. "Yes."

"And couldn't that be what Elise's unhappy spirit is trying to tell you—that it was an accident?"

Mort looked uncomfortable. "Now you're being melodramatic!"

"No, I'm sticking with facts."

"I'll go along with your theory it may have been an accident," the stout man said. "But I won't buy the rest—that her ghost is coming back and trying to tell me so."

"All right," she said. "Wait. I'm sure it's only a matter of time until you see her."

"And I say you need a psychiatrist," Mort said, returning to his first stand.

Their conversation ended at this point. She left him to go up and shower and change into another dress for dinner. But she felt that the time hadn't been wasted. She had pounded away with her questions until she'd finally managed to get the admission from him she'd wanted. She'd always believed that Elise had fallen from the balcony while drunk and depressed. But Mort had veered away from this. Now she'd made him agree that Elise's death could have been an accident rather than suicide.

When she went downstairs, Aunt Madge Carter was presiding over cocktails on the patio. The older woman greeted her and ordered her to join the group. Mort Venn was standing with a drink in his hand and a rather uncomfortable-looking Kay Dunninger sat holding an untouched martini.

"I'm having a whiskey sour," the old woman told Nina. "What do you want?"

"Just some rye on ice with a dash of water," she said.

Aunt Madge gave Mort Venn a dictatorial glare. "Fix it for her, Mr. Venn. You are responsible when Greg isn't here."

"Right away," Mort said and moved over to the sideboard where the drinks and mix had been set out.

Aunt Madge now turned her attention to Nina and said, "I understand you've been out driving around."

"Yes."

"What did you see?" the old woman wanted to know.

"I drove through Dark Harbor and then over to the museum," she said. "I met Captain Zachary Miller and drove him to his cottage. He's a nice old man."

"Typical islander," Aunt Madge said grumpily. "His type doesn't care for us summer people. Thinks we're outsiders."

"He seemed very friendly," Nina said.

"They pretend," was Aunt Madge's opinion. "They make a good deal of money off us. But underneath it all, they'd rather we weren't here."

"I didn't find any of that in him," she said. "He spoke of

your family very warmly. He particularly mentioned Grant."

Aunt Madge's pale face showed a sudden shadow and she stared off into space as she said, "Grant was a favorite on the island. He had a knack of making friends with everyone."

Mort Venn came over and handed her the drink she'd requested. "I think it will be strong enough," he said.

Nina thanked him and said, "I'm sure it will be all right."

Aunt Madge sipped her drink and, returning to what seemed a favorite subject with her, said, "I remember a story my father told about the Pirate Islanders. He said that the local paper ran a long account of a shipwreck in which five sailors were lost. And the way the paper put it was, 'three souls were lost from the island and two New Bedforders.' Father always laughed about that!"

Nina tasted her drink and found it strong and she noticed that Kay still hadn't touched her martini. She asked the girl, "Is there something wrong with your drink?"

Kay looked embarrassed. "No. It's very good. But I hardly ever drink."

Aunt Madge Carter glared at her. "My doctor tells me that an early evening cocktail is medicinal."

Mort chuckled and raised his glass. "Here's to medicine."

Aunt Madge asked Kay, "Did Greg leave you plenty of work to do?"

The girl nodded. "Yes. I'm still behind in my typing."

"That scalawag nephew of mine shouldn't have run off with guests here," the old woman complained. "He had no real need to leave the island overnight. I'm sure of it!"

Morton Venn said placatingly, "I believe it had to do with some people from his New York office visiting in Boston."

"More likely some wild party," Aunt Madge said grimly. She turned to Kay again and said, "You've worked for both my nephews. Don't you find Greg a lot wilder than Grant was?"

Again Kay showed uneasiness. "It's very difficult for me to judge," she said. "I have mostly seen Greg during business hours and it was the same with Grant."

The old woman smiled sourly at this. "A diplomatic reply but hardly a true one. Never mind, I won't put you on the spot. You are a guest in my house."

"And a lovely time it is to be a guest," Mort Venn said. "We have had nothing but fine days."

"The fog and rain will come soon enough, believe me," Aunt Madge said. "We get our share of it." She gave her attention to Nina again and said, "So you met the Cramers and that Bettina Wells today?"

"Yes," she said, wondering what was coming next.

"Bettina Wells is a sly, rather common British type," the old woman said maliciously. "And that daughter can be a vixen for all her pretty face. I was delighted when Grant broke his engagement with her. And as for that man she married— that Val Cramer!" The old woman made a face.

Nina said, "He's a very good artist."

Aunt Madge rolled her eyes. "You've seen his workshop and studio. That dark corridor with the alcoves and all those frightening lifelike effigies! It's the weirdest place I have ever visited."

She smiled faintly. "He has chosen an odd field for his talents, but he is clever."

"An odd field!" the old woman echoed. "The man is downright strange. You must have noticed the brooding, sinister quality about him. And then that Lincoln beard to make him look like a mad version of Honest Abe!"

Mort Venn said, "There's no doubt he is an oddball. But Nina is right. He's also clever and I can't see any harm in him or what he's doing."

Aunt Madge gave Mort a reproving look. "There you and I

disagree. Have you noticed how many of his effigies are of people who have died violently? He has both poor Grant and Elise there you know. I can't bear to look at them."

Nina stared at the old woman. "You can't think there is any connection between his effigies and the way some of his subjects died?"

"It makes me wonder," Aunt Madge said with a brooding light in her pale blue eyes. "He manipulates those effigies like puppets. You wonder if perhaps in making them he didn't cast some grim spell over their lives."

Kay Dunninger spoke up for the first time, in hushed tones. "I believe in the old days practitioners of his craft were accused of that very thing. It was considered a form of black magic."

"That is true," the old woman said. "You'll find it in the books of witchcraft. And I'm not at all sure he isn't up to some sort of wicked tricks."

Nina smiled faintly. "He spoke about that. Of course, people being superstitious of what he's doing makes him angry."

Aunt Madge looked unimpressed. "That still doesn't mean he isn't up to something!"

Mort Venn was standing almost directly behind the old lady and now he made a face for Nina's benefit to warn her not to continue the subject. He was apparently afraid that the old woman would get too worked up.

To change the conversation Nina told Aunt Madge, "I saw the windmill today. In fact I drove up by it. I suppose it must be very old."

"It was built around 1750 and restored by the Historical Society," Aunt Madge said. "From the mill you can see all over the island. Derek Mills takes a great interest in it. Have you met him?"

"Yes. He was here at the cocktail party, wasn't he?" she said.

"That's right! He was. Seems a long while ago to me now," Aunt Madge sighed. "I guess it's a sign of old age that I'm no longer aware of time passing."

Kay Dunninger had taken some furtive sips of her martini and now the dark girl said, "I've always understood that the old are much sharper about time than the young."

"Don't believe it!" Aunt Madge said with a grim look on her pale, jowled face. "Time, like most things, gets sort of fuzzy to ancients like myself. I have to battle constantly to think young."

"But you do think young," Mort Venn complimented her. "And that is why we are all so fond of you."

The old woman grimaced and put down her empty glass. "You won't be fond of me if I keep you late for dinner. It is time to go in. You can take me on your arm, Mort!"

She rose from her chair and the stout man hastened to escort her into the dining room. Nina watched it all with some amusement. Aunt Madge took Mort's arm as if it were her right. The old lady had a great deal of dignity. Nina and Kay followed them to the cool, dark room.

At the table Aunt Madge said grimly, "Our numbers seem to get fewer."

Nina agreed, "I know."

Mort's round face showed a sign of shadow. No doubt he was missing his dead wife. In happier days Elise had often been a guest at Blue Gables. Nina could picture the lovely blonde woman seated at the table. And this brought back visions of the ghost she'd been seeing recently. She had confided in Mort about seeing Elise's ghost and he'd refused to believe it. Perhaps she'd made a mistake to tell him but it seemed that it was something he should know.

The entree, broiled lobster, was excellent, but the conversation was less than brilliant, with Aunt Madge and Mort keeping up most of it. They entered into a discussion of famous old houses on the island, most of which were unknown to Nina.

Her mind wandered and she tried to recall the last time that Elise and Grant had been at this same table together. So much time had passed that it was confusing. She thought it had been on a Columbus Day about two years earlier. Grant had been deep in the planning of his political campaign then and so he and Elise had spent a great deal of time together. It was Elise who'd taken the main part in preparing Grant's campaign. Nina had thought nothing of the two spending so much time in each other's company. It was only later when the scandal and deaths came that she had begun to worry about it.

But even now she still believed that the relationship between the two had been innocent. Mort admitted that he had often had doubts about his wife but Nina had never felt that way about Grant. Still, the newspaper articles linking the blonde woman with Grant had been deadly accurate. And the records of the land scandal had been damning, except that Grant and Elise had not seemed to realize the financial benefits indicated by the newspapers. Was the money hidden away somewhere in secret bank accounts? It was a possibility. But she was not ready to accept this yet.

They came to the end of the meal and left the table and the dining room. Nina went out to stroll in the garden and Mort came out to stroll with her. She would rather have been alone but she did not want to offend him.

He began, "Madge Carter was in a great state at the cocktail hour. I'm glad we steered her away from the superstitious stuff."

Nina said, "I know. She was allowing herself to become

much too bothered about it."

Mort gave her a warning glance. "I hope you haven't said anything to her about seeing Elise's ghost?"

She hesitated. The fact was that the old woman had told her that she'd seen the phantom figure. But she didn't want to tell Mort this. He'd been through enough, it seemed, without harping on ghosts. Evading the question she replied, "I never discuss anything too seriously with her if I can avoid it."

"Good," Mort said. "I'm heartily in agreement with that. Things are not quite the same with Greg away."

"Especially not with our numbers so reduced," she agreed.

"Yes. At other times there were Grant and Elise," Mort Venn said as they strolled on. "I sometimes wonder why I come here at all. I must want to torture myself about losing Elise."

"You have been coming here every summer for some years," she said. "I guess it's probably habit as much as anything else."

"Perhaps," he said. They had come to the end of the gravel walk and now turned and began slowly making their way to Blue Gables again.

"I didn't plan to remain too long," she said. "But somehow I've stayed on."

He gave her a sharp glance from behind his horn-rimmed glasses. "You have a motive which, even though I don't approve of it, I understand. You're trying to dig into Grant's past to prove he was innocent of all that scandal."

"I can't imagine why you don't approve," she protested. "If only for Elise's sake. Don't you want to clear her name?"

"She's dead and so is Grant. Senator Ryan's indictment of them was fairly complete. I don't think it's possible to change the record."

"And I call that negative thinking of the worst sort," she told him.

"We don't agree," he said with a slow, sad smile. "But as I said, I do understand. Though I'd be just as happy if you gave up the project."

"I'm afraid I can't do that, Mort," she said. "I'm sorry."

"So am I," he replied. "I think you're making yourself unhappy in a hopeless situation and others as well. That's too bad."

"I've never wanted to do that. Especially not to you," she said looking up at him with sympathy. "I know how you must feel about Elise."

"It pains me to think about her," he admitted. "And I am a little afraid that instead of helping you'll only keep the scandal boiling longer."

"I hope I have better sense than that," she said.

"I'm not questioning your motives or your judgement. I think you're mistaken about how serious things were between my wife and Grant," he told her. "But you have to do what you feel is right, so I'll say no more."

"Thank you, Mort," she said with feeling.

He left her and she remained in the garden alone. Night was beginning to fall and the garden lay in shadow. Soon the blue of twilight would turn to darkness and the phantoms of Blue Gables would be released again. After her talk with Mort she was feeling troubled and confused. Was she making a mistake in her pursuit of the facts about the scandal? Should she forget it and leave Pirate Island?

She worried about Greg's having gone to the mainland and wondered what his reasons might have been. She did not understand Grant's brother, so often his actions left her puzzled. She and Grant had been suspicious of Greg posing as him in a relationship with Elise. Could she prove that impersonation now?

Nina sat on a bench in the garden and as the night grew

dark amber lights appeared at the windows as the lamps inside were turned on. Once she saw the stately figure of Aunt Madge Carter sweep by a window and with some nostalgia she thought of the happier days when she and Grant had visited the island together. Life had been so much simpler then.

The only thing marring her happiness at that time had been Greg's resentment of her engagement to his brother. Because of this Greg had remained away from the island whenever he knew she and Grant were coming down for a weekend. Still they were unable to avoid an occasional meeting and on some weekends they had been there together.

It seemed strange that Grant had never mentioned his engagement to Jeri Cramer. Why? It was a puzzle. And she hadn't yet made up her mind about Jeri's mother or her husband. Aunt Madge disliked Val Cramer and made no bones about it. Nina didn't feel that strongly, but there was something about the artist which made her uneasy.

She rose from the bench and strolled through the dark night. There were no stars as yet and as she moved a distance from the house everything was in blackness around her. Far below she had a glimpse of Dark Harbor and a reflection of the town's lights in the dark sky, but that was all. Out on the water there were the lights of pleasure craft and an occasional fishing boat.

She walked almost as far as the roadway before she became aware of the sound of footsteps following her. At first she thought she was merely imagining them and then she heard them quite plainly. Worst of all they were catching up to her!

Now she was really afraid and she began to hurry, almost running in her frantic haste to get back to Blue Gables and escape the phantom footsteps.

A voice at her elbow said, "You needn't be in such a hurry!"

She recognized the man's voice as one she'd heard before without knowing who it was. She twisted her head in an effort to glance over her shoulder and keep hurrying at the same time. As a result she stumbled without catching a glimpse of her pursuer.

"Careful," the male voice said again as he grasped her by the arm and helped restore her balance.

Feeling awkward and a trifle silly she said, "Thank you!"

The male figure loomed over her in the dark. "You still don't remember me?"

"No, I'm afraid I don't," she admitted, thoroughly scared.

"Val Cramer," he said.

"Of course," she gasped, feeling a bit easier. "I knew I'd heard your voice before but I couldn't think where."

"So you ran!" his tone was mocking.

"Yes, I ran," she agreed. "I'm sorry I was so stupid. But I find this place and the island rather frightening these days."

The tall man was a little slow in replying, "Because of losing your fiancé?"

"That wasn't pleasant. Nor were the circumstances of his death," she said.

"I remember. He was drowned after a road accident. On his way here, wasn't he?"

"Yes."

"Well, you mustn't hold it against the island," he said. "We aren't all that bad."

"I'll try and remember that," she said. She glanced up. "There are no stars."

"No. And yet it's very warm. Perhaps we may be due for a thunder-storm."

"Do you think so?"

"Hard to be sure. The signs are in the air."

She said, "You're a long way from the studio, aren't you?"

"Not really," the tall man said. "The studio is almost directly across from where we're standing. I can find my way across the field on any kind of night."

"So it holds no fears for you?"

"No," the tall man said. "I seek inspiration in the darkness. My best ideas often come to me in the night."

"And who is minding the studio?"

"Bettina, my mother-in-law," he said. "We only keep open until nine so she will have closed it by now."

She stood there, still ill at ease. Then she asked, "Would you care to come in for a drink?"

"No, thanks," he said. "Not just now. I'm going to walk back to the studio and call on the muse again. I may still hit on some inspiration." He then said goodnight and left her. His leaving was as abrupt as his intrusion on her had been.

She walked back to the house somewhat relaxed. And she decided she would change into her bathing suit and take a late night swim. It was hot and she felt this might refresh her and make her more ready for sleep.

The strange young artist's explanation for being near the house had been logical enough, and yet it left her uneasy. She made her way into the house and upstairs to her room without seeing anyone. It appeared that the others had retired for the night. After slipping on her bathing suit she came back down again wearing a lace robe over it.

By the pool she discarded the robe and poised to dive in when she thought she saw the shadow of someone moving at the other end of the pool. A chill of fear ran through her and she froze where she was, staring into the darkness.

Chapter Five

Nina hesitated as she peered into the shadows at the other end of the swimming pool. For a moment she had been certain she'd seen someone moving but now there wasn't a hint of anyone. A single small spotlight at her end of the pool illuminated the diving board and the surrounding area, but its light did not reach the other end of the long pool.

At last she decided she'd been wrong and dived into the cool water. She felt thoroughly refreshed after a few minutes and continued to swim back and forth along the length of the pool. When she tired of this she stood up in the dark, shallow end and gazed around her, but there seemed to be no one.

She struck out in the water again and swam toward the lighted, diving-board end of the pool. When she was about three-quarters of the way there she suddenly glanced up and saw a figure moving in the darkness just beyond the glow from the spotlight. She felt herself tense as she struggled to keep afloat and watch the progress of the figure.

Then he stepped out into the partial glow of the spotlight and she saw that it was Greg! He'd returned from the mainland and was behaving in a very odd fashion, not looking at her at all but staring straight ahead of him.

She called out, "Greg! When did you get back?"

He gave her a quick, frightened glance, then backed away into the shadows and vanished. It was a baffling and frustrating performance as far as Nina was concerned. She felt angry at him for refusing to answer. She swam on toward the end of the pool.

She'd almost reached the end of the pool when she suddenly had the distinct sensation that someone was in the pool with her. This on top of her encounter with Greg thoroughly upset her. She glanced fearfully over her shoulder for a sign of someone but there was no one in sight.

Then without warning someone grasped her around the knees and dragged her screaming below the surface. She fought to save herself from her unknown attacker without success. She felt her lungs would burst as she tried to free herself and rise to the surface. But it was no use. She was trapped! Someone was diabolically holding her under water until she drowned. This was her last conscious thought before she blacked out.

When she came to she was on her back on the grass by the diving board end of the pool. Bending over her and trying to help was Bettina Wells. The middle-aged Bettina was in a bathing suit and there was a terrified expression on her face.

She said, "Thank Heavens. I thought I'd lost you!"

Memory returning, she sat up on her elbow with a taut look on her pretty face, "The pool!"

"Take it easy," Bettina said. "I know about the pool. I came to have a late swim and found you in it. You were unconscious and I had all I could do to get you out."

Terror still welled high in her as she exclaimed, "You don't understand! Someone sneaked into the pool behind me, grabbed me and tried to drown me. They held me under water until I blacked out."

Bettina said, "I don't know what happened. I only know you were at the point of drowning when I found you."

"Where is Greg?" she asked anxiously.

"I don't know. Didn't he go to the mainland overnight on business?" Bettina asked.

"He came back. I saw him just before I was drawn under the water."

Bettina eyed her oddly. "Are you sure?"

"Of course I'm sure!" she said. "And I have you to thank for saving my life."

"I'm glad I happened along."

"Someone tried to murder me," Nina went on.

Bettina looked skeptical. "You really mean that?"

"Of course I do," she said. "You found me near death in the water."

"It's true. And I didn't know how you'd managed to get there," she said. "But you were in bad shape."

She sat up fully and ran a hand speculatively down her cheek. "I didn't get a look at who it was."

"Sure you just didn't get panicky and go under on your own?" the older woman asked.

"No!"

Bettina made a placating gesture. "I only suggested it. I don't know what happened."

Nina got to her feet. "I'm going inside," she said.

"Not alone," the other woman said solicitously. "I'll see you in safely."

"I'll be all right. Sorry to spoil your swim."

"That's not important," Bettina said. "I had enough just dragging you out." She had a robe with her which she now put on.

Nina felt weak and ill as she started to walk to the house. Even with Bettina at her side to steady her it was a trying experience. They reached the front entrance and went inside and she collapsed in the first chair she came to in the reception hall.

A figure appeared on the stairway. It was Mort Venn in an enormous wine-red dressing gown. His hair was rumpled as if he'd just risen from bed and his glasses were missing. He halted part way down the stairs.

"What's going on?" he wanted to know.

"First we can do with some brandy," Bettina told him. "This girl has had a narrow escape."

Mort Venn gave a small groan. "More complications?" And he came down and went to the sideboard in the living room to get the brandy.

She looked up at Bettina weakly. "You shouldn't have bothered him."

"Why not?" the middle-aged British woman demanded with a look of indignation. "He has a right to help."

Mort returned with a glass full of brandy. "That's a good snort. Drink it all down at a gulp if you can," he advised.

"I'll strangle," she said, taking the glass.

"Hold your breath," he said.

"I've already had a session of that and I didn't like it," she grimaced. And she made an attack on the brandy, taking a big gulp at first, choking over it, then trying again. She paused with some still in the glass. "I do better taking it by easy stages."

"Whatever you like," he said. "My room is over the pool. I was sure I heard voices and so I came down."

Bettina gave him one of her sly smiles. "I'll bet you heard me and couldn't resist coming down!"

Mort looked annoyed. "As a matter of fact it was Nina's voice I heard and she sounded as if she were in some sort of trouble."

"She was," the British woman said as Nina finished the brandy.

Mort frowned. "Now am I going to be told about it?"

"Yes," Nina said, a trifle revived after the brandy. "I decided to take a late swim in the pool."

Mort glanced at Bettina in her robe and bathing suit. "Seems to have been a popular idea."

"Lucky for me that it was," she said. "I thought I saw someone at the dark end of the pool before I got in. Then I decided I was wrong. So I dived in and swam for a while."

"Then what?" Mort wanted to know.

She said, "I was swimming toward the deep end of the pool when I saw a man in the shadows. He came forward and it was Greg."

"Greg!" Mort said in astonishment.

"Yes."

"He's not on the island tonight," Mort said.

"That's what I told her," Bettina joined in.

Nina looked up at them both in dismay. "But he must have come back without anyone knowing. I saw him."

"We'll check that later," the stout man said. "Go on."

"After that everything happened swiftly," she said. "I was swimming and suddenly someone under water grabbed me and dragged me down. They kept me under until I became unconscious. And if Bettina hadn't happened along I'd have drowned."

Mort's moon face showed amazement. "Are you saying someone slipped into the pool without you knowing it and tried to drown you?"

"Yes!"

"It doesn't seem possible," Mort said, dismissing the idea.

"But it's exactly what happened," she protested.

"You didn't get a look at him at all?" Mort's eyes were questioning.

"No," she said.

"That's some story," he said in a skeptical tone.

Bettina spoke up, "I think she's telling the truth. She was in the water unconscious when I found her."

"And I'm a good swimmer," Nina reminded him.

Mort looked bemused. "It's a pretty wild story. I don't know what to make of it. And then this other business about Greg."

"I saw him!" she insisted.

Mort said, "I'll go up and take a look in his room."

"He won't be there," she protested. "I saw him outside."

Mort gave her an expressionless look. "He could be there now. He's had time. I'll take a look." And the big man wearily trudged back up the stairs.

Bettina gave her a warning look. "I'm afraid you're not going to get much help in that direction. He has no imagination to speak of."

"He'll not find Greg up there," she agreed. "Just the same I know he's back. There was no mistaking him."

Bettina was standing in the shadowed reception hall and studying Nina with an odd expression on her plain face. And in a taut voice, she said, "Unless—"

"Unless what?"

Bettina's tone was solemn. "Unless you saw Grant's ghost."

"Grant's ghost!" The impact of the woman's words hit her like a clenched fist.

"Yes."

"You don't mean that!"

"Why not?"

"I know it was Greg. Not any ghost!" she protested.

Bettina looked knowing. "What did Greg have on?"

"I didn't notice!"

"You saw only his face?"

"Mostly. It was shadowed. I couldn't make out any details of what he was wearing."

"Sounds more and more like a ghost, my dear," Bettina

said in a voice of somber authority.

"Don't torment me!" she protested.

The older woman's eyes met hers. "I'm simply making you see the truth."

"By telling me I saw Grant's ghost?" she demanded angrily. "I don't believe in ghosts!"

"I wonder."

She stared at the woman. "You are deliberately torturing me, aren't you?"

"You've had a very weird experience," Bettina said. "I'm trying to get to the bottom of it."

"You needn't go far," she said unhappily. "Someone who wants me to stop the investigation tried to drown me."

"I see it from a ghostly angle, I'm sorry," Bettina said in a reproving tone.

The exchange between them was interrupted by the appearance of Mort Venn on the stairway again. He came down to join them with a lugubrious expression on his round face. He said, "I've been to Greg's room. He's not there and his bag isn't there. I'd say he's still on the mainland."

"And I say I saw him!" Nina insisted.

Mort looked forlorn. "I guess we could go on arguing that point all night."

Nina said, "He could easily still be here on the island."

Mort said, "I guess we'll have to wait until morning to know that. I think you ought to go to bed and try and get some sleep."

"I will," she said.

"Now!" Mort said firmly.

"You needn't wait," she told him. "I'll go in a minute."

Mort looked at Bettina. "What about you?"

"What about me?" the British woman asked.

"How are you going to get home?" he asked.

"No problem," she said. "I have a flashlight and I'm used to walking across the field late at night."

The big man smiled maliciously. "You mean to say you aren't afraid of the phantoms?"

"No," Bettina said.

"You'd better be if Nina is right," he said with sarcasm. "She spots a new ghost every night."

"If she claims she sees them then I believe her," Bettina replied boldly.

Mort didn't look pleased. He said, "If I remember correctly you always had some sort of argument going at the office. We rarely agreed."

"I don't see that is important now," Bettina said.

He grunted. "No, but I think it's significant. I'm too sleepy for ghost stories. I'll say goodnight to you both." And with that he made his way up the stairs again.

When he was out of hearing range Bettina said, "Now there's a sweet, sympathetic character!"

Nina got up. "I don't suppose you can blame him. It is late and I did wake him from a sound sleep."

"Too bad!" the older woman said with disgust.

"I'm going to bed," she said, and gave the British woman a concerned look. "You're sure you'll be safe going back to the studio?"

"Of course I will," Bettina said in her bluff way. "I'll see you tomorrow. And next time we're together I want to read your palm. I'm certain what I see there will help explain a lot."

"I'm not interested in fortune telling," she protested.

The British woman gave her a bland look. "You'd better be. I have a notion you're going to need some sound advice."

Nina saw her to the door. Bettina stepped out into the dark night without a hint of fear or hesitation. Nina closed the door after her and locked it. She could not help but have a good deal of admiration for the courageous woman. At the same time she had the feeling there was something sinister about her. She did not know whether she should trust her even though she had apparently saved her life.

Nina thought about this and came to a troubled question. Could it be that the British woman had not only been her rescuer but her attacker as well? Had she given up the attack because she felt she'd been seen and then quickly changed to the role of rescuer?

It was a frightening thought and she tried to dismiss it. But someone had tried to drown her and it had not been a ghost. The mystery of Greg still remained to be explained. Again she asked herself if he might have made his way into the pool and attacked her. For despite what Mort thought, she was sure she had seen him. The suggestion Bettina had made that she might have seen Grant's ghost was too much!

With these thoughts in mind she went up to her bedroom. It was not surprising that for most of the night she was plagued by nightmares. Weird dreams in which she was stalked by phantom figures. She awoke in the morning feeling weary.

She expected to see Greg somewhere downstairs. But there was no sign of him. During the night the fog had moved in and it was a dull gray day with the mist thick in the island air. The only person at the breakfast table was Kay Dunninger.

Nina at once asked the dark girl, "Did Greg come home last night?"

Kay showed surprise. "No. Was he supposed to?"

"I thought he might have," she said. "I was sure I saw him walking across the lawn last night."

"As far as I know he isn't here yet," the girl said. "And I imagine the morning ferry will be late with the fog so bad."

"Yes, it is a thick fog," she agreed, worried about whether

Greg had returned or not. There could be no question that she'd seen him or his likeness. And if it had been his likeness then Bettina Wells was right. She'd seen a ghost—Grant's ghost!

Kay finished her coffee. "I must get back to my typing," she said. "I still have quite a lot to do."

Nina asked her, "Do you like working for Greg as much as you did working for Grant?"

Kay said quietly, "They're two very different people."

"Even though they look alike," she agreed.

"Yes," the dark girl said. "The resemblance ends there."

"I've been thinking about it. Probably you and I knew Grant as well as anyone and we both know Greg. I was engaged to him before I met Grant."

The girl's plain face showed interest. "I've heard that. You really liked Grant better?"

"Of course. Didn't you?"

Kay looked flustered. "My position isn't quite the same as yours. I'm merely an employee."

"You've been with the family long enough to be regarded as something more than that," she chided her.

"I have found qualities in both men," Kay said. "Perhaps Greg is a bit more headstrong and selfish than his late brother."

"Much more so."

"That's the main difference."

"And an important one," she said. She gave the dark girl a searching look. "Do you think the stories spread about Grant and Elise had any truth in them?"

Kay looked almost panicky. "I wouldn't like to say."

"I think you feel as I do, that they were purely political garbage. Lies made up to hurt Grant and Elise, especially Grant. They were merely getting at him through her."

Kay nodded. "Once she killed herself there wasn't much hope of finding out the truth."

"I don't think she did kill herself," Nina said, looking directly at the girl.

Kay looked astonished. "What do you mean?"

"I think she was drinking and fell accidentally."

Kay said, "I suppose it could have been that. The inquest proved she'd had a lot to drink. But sometimes people about to kill themselves bolster their courage with alcohol."

"I don't believe that is what happened. I think she drank because she was troubled and then stumbled and fell over that balcony railing."

"Have you any way of proving it?"

"Not yet."

"I hope you will be able to clear Grant's name," Kay said, rising. "He was very nice to me."

"I'm sure he was."

The dark girl stood there awkwardly for a moment, then she said, "Well, my work is waiting. Excuse me." And she almost ran out of the room.

Nina finished her breakfast. She was disappointed that Kay had not been of more help to her. But the girl was so determined to be a scrupulously correct employee that she rarely voiced an opinion on anything despite her above-average intelligence.

As Nina left the dining room she came face to face with Mort Venn. The advertising man, his hair combed neatly, his glasses on and wearing a neat gray summer suit looked little like the rumpled character in the dressing gown.

He smiled at her and said, "What did you do to Kay, she came hurrying out of the dining room like a frightened deer!"

She shrugged. "I tried to ask her a few questions and she seemed to panic."

"You should know she's very high-strung."

"I tend to forget," she admitted bleakly.

He gave her an amused look. "Have any more exciting adventures last night?"

"No. Don't you think I had enough?"

"Sorry," he said. "I didn't mean to sound as if I were making a joke of it."

"It sounded very much like that."

The big man said, "If you think someone really did try to drown you, it might be a good idea to call in the Pirate Island police."

She said, "The local constabulary consists of one officer, named Titus Frink. If I decide to go to the police I think I'll phone the State Police on the Cape."

"That probably would be wise," he said, much more soberly.

He went into the living room and she went upstairs to get her raincoat. She had a familiar desire to get away from the old mansion. When she came back down, she encountered Aunt Madge making her way upstairs.

The old woman glanced at her raincoat and asked, "Where in the world are you going in this awful fog? If it's sightseeing, you might as well save your time. You can't see ten yards in front of you."

"I'm just anxious to get some air," she said.

"You'll find it damp," Aunt Madge predicted. "And if you drive you'd better take care. There's an awful lot of motor accidents on the island in this weather."

"I'll keep that in mind," she said. "Have you seen Greg this morning?"

"Certainly not," Aunt Madge snapped as if this were the worst of silly questions. "He'll be late. The ferry is always delayed in this weather."

She said, "I had an idea he came home last evening."

"Nonsense. He made it very plain he'd be on the mainland all night," Aunt Madge sputtered and went on by her up the stairs.

As Nina made her way down she considered this. It was true that Greg had insisted he'd planned to remain in Boston overnight. He'd done so in such a deliberate fashion she wondered whether he wasn't trying to establish an alibi. She was sure she'd seen him and yet everyone else assumed, because of what he'd said, that he'd not come back. It could be that was what he was counting on.

She went out into the foggy morning and discovered that the old woman was right. Everything was shrouded in fog and you could not make out the distant trees or any part of the landscape. It was all a gray void. Strolling slowly she came to the pool and stared at it. She still trembled at the remembrance of how close she had come to death in there.

Could Greg have returned surreptitiously in the night with a plan to kill her? It might very well be that he wanted her out of the way. She and Grant had gradually arrived at the suspicion it was Greg and Elise who had been carrying on a torrid affair for which Grant had taken the blame. For that reason Greg might want to see her dead.

But his motive could go deeper than that. He and Elise might well have put their hands on the money made from the fraudulent land deal. And if they had, he must surely have full control of it now with Elise dead. There would be no one he need share it with. His only danger lay in Nina's connecting him with Elise and the swindle. And Greg knew she was on the island for just that reason.

When would Greg show himself? Likely not until after the ferry had been in for a while. Then he would appear at the house and pretend that he had just returned from the mainland. She would need convincing proof of this after all that had happened. She was loath to admit that she had seen a ghost. Especially as there was also the mystery of the attack on her to be explained.

In the distance a foghorn blared its melancholy warning. She could well imagine how dangerous the sea would be on such a day. There were many risky shoals near the island making the area hard to navigate even in good weather. No wonder the ferry from the Cape would be delayed.

Still restless, she decided to risk taking a drive. The receptionist at the museum had said that Derek Mills would be there all day and she had a sudden desire to see the pleasant young man and talk to him. With this in mind she started her car.

The engine of the small sports car was damp and it took her a few minutes to get underway properly. But as soon as the powerful little motor warmed up she had no trouble. No trouble except for the visibility. She had to drive at an agonizingly low speed and she once missed a turn and had to retrace her way to get on the proper road which led across the island.

As she drew a little distance from the shore to the higher point of the island there was a slight easing of the fog. She could barely make out the museum building as she pulled up to it. She was pleased to note there were few tourist cars parked there on this bleak day, so she hoped Derek Mills would not be too busy.

She went inside and was quickly ushered up to his private office on the second floor. As she went in she discovered him seated at his desk making some entries in a large ledger. He glanced up and when he saw it was her a pleased look came over his bronzed face.

Looking every inch the Pirate Island aristocrat in his gray

flannel suit, button-down collar and conservative tie, he waved her to a chair and said, "I'm glad to see you, Miss Patton. Sorry I missed you when you called yesterday."

"It didn't matter," she said, seating herself.

He sat back and studied her admiringly. "You deserve a medal for courage, driving on a day like this. The visibility must be zero."

"Or close to it," she said. "I remembered our talk at the cocktail party the other night and I found myself wanting to see you again."

"I like the sound of that, Miss Patton."

"Nina, please," she said.

He smiled. "Very well, Nina."

"I'm here with a problem," she told him.

"I'm glad you decided to bring it to me," he said.

She glanced toward the open door to the hall. "Would you mind if I closed the door?"

"Let me do it," he said, already on his feet to shut the door. He then came back and stood before her. "I take it you have something sensational to discuss with me."

"Yes."

"Fire away," the young man said.

She quickly told him of the ghostly figures she'd seen at Blue Gables in the night. And of the vicious attack in the pool.

"It's only luck that I'm alive," she said, winding up her story.

Derek Mills had listened to it all with stern attention. When she finished, he said, "You've told me a very strange story."

"I promise it's true."

"I'm not disputing it," he hurried to say. "I'm just trying to see if I can make some sense of it."

"I doubt it," she said wryly.

"I can try," he said. "In the beginning you saw only the ghostly figure of Elise?"

"Yes. And Greg's Aunt Madge saw it also."

"Ah," Derek said. "So we have more than one witness if we can get them to testify."

"That's right," she agreed. "And I'm sure she will talk if you approach her correctly."

The young museum curator gave her a warning glance. "You mustn't think I have any legal power in a matter like this. It is strictly up to the island police and I trust that Titus Frink might be able to handle it. Though knowing him, I doubt it."

With a worried expression, she said, "I don't want to put it into the hands of the police until I have some idea who my deadly enemy may be."

"Does that matter?" the pleasant young man asked.

"Yes, it does," she said. "I would like to get my facts straight before I contact the police. I think it's a continuation of the dirty campaign they waged against Grant."

Derek Mills frowned in remembering. "I know all about that campaign. I thought it disgraceful."

"I'm glad."

"No question about it," he said. "And you are now thinking that Greg may have taken part in the vicious attacks on his brother and be desperately anxious to conceal it?"

"Yes."

"You say you saw Greg just before you were attacked last night?"

"I did," she agreed. "And I wonder if he didn't return to the island early and make the attempt on my life."

"He's a good swimmer," Derek said.

"It was a good swimmer who remained under water and tried to drown me."

93

"So it may have been Greg," Derek agreed. "On the other hand it could have been that British woman, Bettina Wells!"

"That's worried me also," she admitted. "What do you know about her?"

"Not much. She came here with the Cramers when they bought that property from Madge Carter. I never could understand the Carters selling their guest cottage and the barn with it. They surely didn't need the money."

"Perhaps the cottage was empty most of the time and they felt it would be better in use," she suggested.

"That's very likely it," he said. "Val Cramer is a good artist but a strange one. And I think his wife, Jeri, and her mother are a little offbeat. But that doesn't mean there's anything wrong with them."

"Of course not," she said seriously.

"Many people are strange and in no way dangerous," the museum director went on.

"I know that," she said. "It is only because of last night I'm truly suspicious. Bettina was there when I came to. What worries me is whether she is also the one who tried to drown me and either lost her nerve or thought she'd been seen by Greg. If she was my attacker, for some reason she decided to save me."

"I can follow your reasoning," Derek said. "And you are right not to rule out that woman. After all she was employed by the Venn agency in that campaign. And while she was supposedly working for your fiancé she could have been giving away secrets of their plans to his opponents."

"Yes," she agreed.

Derek sat with his hands folded on the desk before him. "But before you can ask the police to take a hand you have to have more than supposition."

"A lot depends on whether Greg was on the island last night," she said.

"Even then you'd need proof to convict him of any attack on you."

"I know that," she agreed. "But you need to establish one thing at a time. Then build."

The young man nodded. "I hope I can help. Let's try the ferry house and see if the ferry has arrived from the mainland."

"She should have been in long ago."

"Not in this fog," he said. "I know the captain well and I'll ask him about Greg."

She sat quietly while he gave the operator a number and put through the call. Then he asked if the ferry had made its morning trip and she judged that the answer was yes. He next asked to speak to the ferry's captain. There was a moment's delay and he gave her an encouraging nod.

"She's been in for about twenty minutes," he said. Then he gave his attention to the phone again. "Is that you Captain? This is Derek. I hear you had a hard trip. I can imagine. Can you tell me something? I'd like to know if Greg Carter was a passenger on this morning's trip."

Nina stared at the young man as he listened to the reply from the other end of the line and tried to tell what the answer was from the expression on his face. It was difficult to decide, she thought as her heart pounded with excitement.

Chapter Six

Derek Mills finally put down the phone and gave her a sober look. He said, "Greg was on the ferry this morning. He talked with the captain during the trip over."

She stared at the young man in the gray flannel suit in dismay. "You're sure?"

"No question of it."

She considered. "So that means?"

"Either you must have been mistaken last night or you saw a ghost," Derek Mills said quietly.

She tried to hide her panic without much success. There was a tremor in her voice as she said, "That doesn't give me much choice, does it?"

"I'm afraid not," he said.

Nina thought hard. "I'm sure I saw Greg. I remember his face standing out against the darkness clearly."

"All you saw was his face?"

"I think so."

"You could have been mistaken. You were in a highly nervous state," he suggested. "I wouldn't be too upset about this."

"I'm afraid I can't help being upset," she said unhappily.

"Are you going to challenge Greg about it?"

She sighed. "What can I say? He was definitely on board the ferry this morning. That means he couldn't have been here on the island last night."

"Exactly," Derek said. "I'd say you might be wise to say nothing to Greg about this for the present. It may be that later you'll find some clues to what really went on."

"That could be good advice," she said.

"The best I can offer."

"I shouldn't have bothered you with my problems," she said. "I'm sorry."

Derek Mills smiled. "Not at all. I'm glad you did come to me. And I'll want to talk with you again. When will we have a chance to meet?"

"I don't know. Almost anytime. That is as long as I decide to remain on the island."

The young man at once looked worried. "Then you're actually thinking of leaving?"

Nina spread a hand in a gesture. "I don't think I've made up my mind," she said. "I'm almost sure someone wants to kill me to stop my digging up the scandal concerning Grant and Elise. But I don't know who. And I'm not sure that running away from the island will solve my problems."

"Running away from problems is seldom helpful," Derek Mills said.

"If I stay here I may be making myself a target for a killer."

"But isn't that also your best chance of bringing this killer out into the open?"

"Perhaps," she admitted.

"Not that I like all this talk of killing," Derek Mills said. "Are you really serious about it? If so, isn't it a matter for the police?"

"So far it's all speculation on my part," she said. "I doubt if the police would listen to me. They'd consider me a silly female imagining things."

The young man frowned. "Is there anything I can do?"

She mustered a forlorn smile for him. "Keep in touch with

me. I'm liable to need a friend."

"You have my promise of that," he said earnestly. "Suppose we have dinner together some night soon. There are some pretty decent places on the island. I can phone you."

"I'll count on that," she said.

"Good," Derek Mills said. And then with a rather nervous smile, he asked, "I won't be offending Greg in any way by asking you out, will I?"

"No," she said. "It was his brother to whom I was engaged, not Greg. He has no ties on me." And she got up to leave.

"Excellent," Derek Mills said. "I just wanted to be sure. I'd hate to create any ill will." He saw her to the door.

"Your phone call will be welcome at any time," she said.

"Be careful on the drive back," the young man warned her. "All the ordinary traffic hazards are doubled on a day like this."

She left the museum with his warning fresh in her ears and drove slowly in the direction of Blue Gables. The visit with Derek Mills had been both rewarding and troubling. To have the assurance of his friendship was definitely a plus, but through him she'd found that Greg had not been on the island when she'd thought she'd seen him, and this was a definite let-down.

He had been right when he said she had either allowed her nerves to trick her into making a mistake or she had seen a ghost. The ghost of Grant, of course. Old Captain Zachary Miller had suggested that the souls of drowned men whose bodies are not found continue to wander their familiar haunts on earth. The idea sent a shudder through her as she drove on through the thick fog. The question which now tormented her was whether she had truly seen a ghost or not.

She was so occupied with these thoughts that she gave a little less attention to her driving than she should have in the dense fog. She came to a crossroads and halted for what she thought was a sufficient time and then drove on in the thick gray mist which even car headlights could not penetrate.

She'd gone barely any distance when she was suddenly aware of a car heading directly toward her. The driver had lost his sense of direction and was now over on the wrong side of the road and coming at quite a speed. She screamed and recognized Mort Venn at the wheel of the larger car and by the look of horror on his face, he'd realized his error too late.

The crash came and with it she sank into a black void. She floated in this state, blissfully unaware of anything, for some time. Then she became conscious of a throbbing pain in her head and wearily opened her eyes. She was in a small, white, unfamiliar room.

She had a dreadful headache and she was neatly tucked in bed. She did not understand it. She was about to cry out when the door of the room opened and a jocular, elderly man with white hair and rosy cheeks came in to join her.

He came straight over to her and said, "I'm Dr. Henry Taylor. You're in my private hospital. Don't tell me you don't like it since I only opened it six months ago and it is my particular pride."

She listened to him rather painfully without fully understanding all he said, as she asked, "What am I doing here?"

Dr. Henry Taylor stood by her bedside. "You were in a car accident. Remember?"

She tried to ignore her throbbing head and think. Then it began to come back to her. The car moving through the gray mist and next the other larger car coming head-on toward her. And Mort Venn had been at the wheel of it!

She gave the doctor a frightened look. "Mort Venn struck me head-on with his big car!"

"Fine! That's excellent! You're exactly right. And that

proves you had nothing more than a bad blow on the head rather than a serious concussion, as I feared at first."

"Was anyone else hurt?" she asked, attempting to sit up in bed.

Dr. Taylor restrained her. Easing her back on the pillow, he said, "Now just take it easy. Don't try to move around too much or sit up. You need to be very quiet if you're to come through this without harm."

She gave a deep, dejected sigh and stared up at him, "I can't even sit up?"

"Not just yet. You've a good-sized bump on the left side of your head. Luckily your hair will cover it or you'd be quite a sight for a few days. If you'll keep quiet I may discharge you in the morning. Otherwise, I don't know."

She gave him a forlorn smile. "You just want to use your hospital!"

The ruddy-faced old doctor chuckled. "Now who knows but that you may be right? I'm not going to let you get away easily, be sure of that."

"Was Mort hurt?" she asked.

"Just shaken up," the old man in the white jacket said. "He was very worried about you."

"We're friends," she said. "We're both guests of the Carters."

"So I was given to understand."

"What time is it?"

"You mustn't worry about time. Relax," the doctor said.

"Can't you tell me? I'm curious as to how long I've been unconscious," she said.

"It's after six," Dr. Henry Taylor said. "You've been out of it for quite a few hours. But you seem to have survived in first-class shape."

"I don't feel first-class."

"You won't for a while. By the morning your head will be better."

"Everything is so confused. What about the cars?" she asked.

"I can't tell you a thing," the doctor said. "I know they towed them away. I was only concerned about you and that other fellow who was driving."

"Naturally," she said.

"I'll see that my wife brings you some beef broth," the old doctor said with a smile. "She's a nurse and my main help at the present."

"How many patients do you have here?"

"You're the only one at the moment," he said. "We don't want any more as my regular nurse is on the mainland on holiday."

Nina smiled. "It's a new experience. Having a hospital all to myself."

"The hospital is only a six-room annex off my office," Dr. Taylor said. "Even if it were full, the patient total would be light."

The doctor left her and she lay alone in the antiseptic, white room mulling over her thoughts. She'd been on her way back from the museum when she'd been hit by Mort Venn's car. The large model he was driving must have made a mess of her smaller vehicle. At least he hadn't been hurt. That was something to be thankful for.

She'd left the museum stunned by the information that Greg had actually been on the mainland for the night. She was sure she'd seen him in the dark by the swimming pool, or perhaps it had been a ghost as had been suggested. She knew she'd seen the phantom figure of Elise Venn earlier; now it seemed a ghostly Grant was at large on the old estate.

The doctor's wife came with a tray. She sat for a moment

while Nina took the broth. When she'd finished, Nina said, "I feel much better."

"That's good," the doctor's wife, a pleasant middle-aged woman, said. "You're going to have two visitors shortly. And if you give your word not to excite yourself, I'm sure the doctor will allow them in for a little."

"You have my word," she said. "My head feels better already. Who is coming to see me?"

"Greg Carter and that artist's wife, Jeri Cramer is her name, I believe," the doctor's wife said as she stood by the door with the tray in her hands.

"Of, yes, of course," Nina said. "I'll be glad to see them. Do let them come in."

"I'll tell the doctor," was all that the woman would promise.

Nina sank back on her pillow and thought about her visitors. She found it interesting and provocative that Greg and Jeri should call on her together. She had no idea that they saw that much of each other. Of course she knew that Jeri had once been engaged to Grant. But that had been long ago before she was married. Was she now carrying on an affair with his look-alike brother?

She was thinking about this and other things when Dr. Henry Taylor returned. Cherubic and efficient in his white jacket, he took her pulse and asked her a few questions. Then he said, "A couple outside is waiting to see you."

"You will let them in," she pleaded.

"I'll give you a half-hour and no longer," the doctor warned her. "After that I'm going to give you a sedative to make you sleep until morning. You don't seem to understand that you were injured and you do need rest."

"Anything you say, doctor. Just let me see my visitors."

He smiled. "You're lucky I'm so liberal. Some doctors

wouldn't think of allowing anyone in here until tomorrow at the least."

"You said you'd be discharging me tomorrow," she reminded him.

"Only if you show progress. And if you don't obey my orders, there won't be any progress," the old doctor said.

"You don't have to bully me," she told him.

He laughed and went outside. A moment later he ushered Greg and Jeri into the room with admonitions not to upset her. When the doctor left them, Greg came over and took her hand in his.

His handsome face, so like Grant's she thought, was solemn. "I was terrified that you might have been killed," he said.

"It wasn't good driving weather, was it?" she said, trying to keep it light.

"It was dreadful driving weather for anyone not familiar with the island," he said. "If I'd been at home I wouldn't have allowed you to take the car."

"I didn't think it would be so bad," she said.

From the other side of the bed Jeri Cramer smiled at her. The pert, dark-haired girl said, "I came along just in case you might need a lawyer."

"I might at that," she said. "As I remember it Mort Venn was driving on the wrong side of the road."

"He admits it," Jeri said. "You'll have no legal problem there. He's filled with remorse, all two-hundred-and-forty-odd pounds of him!"

"That's right," Greg told her. "Mort admits he was completely to blame."

"What about the cars?" she asked.

Greg said, "Yours is a complete wreck and his is pretty badly smashed up but it can be fixed. His insurance will take care of you."

Jeri said, "Just as long as you are all right."

"Dr. Taylor says I am. He hopes I'll be able to leave here tomorrow."

"I wouldn't rush it," Greg said.

"I won't," she promised. "I'm sure he won't allow it. He seems a very good doctor."

"He is," Greg said.

Jeri said, "Val told me he met you last night. You were both walking in the fog."

"Yes. I should have kept on walking. But I became restless this morning and decided to drive to the museum."

"You should have waited," Greg said.

"I know that now," Nina agreed.

He frowned. "And Mort was foolish taking his car out as well. He doesn't know the island any better than you do."

"I'm sure we were all restless," she said.

"Yes," Greg said, his handsome face shadowed. "According to what Mort told me, some strange things happened at Blue Gables last night. At least you had some weird experiences."

She felt her cheeks warm and tried to hide her embarrassment. She saw that Jeri was listening with lively curiosity and she resented having this rather intimate business discussed in front of a stranger. She had, on Derek's advice, intended not to mention the episode of seeing the phantom face or the attack on her in the swimming pool. Now it seemed that Mort Venn had taken the matter into his own hands by telling Greg while she was still unconscious in the hospital. It was a nasty complication of her accident.

She said, "It's not all that important. We can talk about it later."

Greg said, "I'm very upset by what Mort told me. I can't think who would want to make such an attack on you."

"I know," she said lamely.

"As soon as you're back at Blue Gables I want to discuss this at length," he told her.

"That would be best," she said. She glanced at them both and told them, "I suppose you'd better go or the doctor will come storming in here."

Jeri smiled and said, "Mother and Val send their best. And by the way, Mother is very anxious to read your palm."

"I'll remember that," she said.

Greg promised, "I'll be in constant touch with the doctor. As soon as he gives permission I'll come over and get you."

"Thanks," she said. "I'm sorry to be such a bother."

"No bother at all," Greg told her. "And you'll be glad to hear the fog has vanished."

Jeri grimaced. "But it will come back. Be sure of that."

Greg gave her a brotherly kiss on the forehead and the two left her. A few minutes later Dr. Taylor came in and gave her the sedative he'd mentioned. He closed the drapes at the windows and turned out the lights. Left in darkness she waited for the drug to work.

She was thinking of Greg and Jeri being together and wondering if it had any significance. From the beginning she'd been interested in Jeri's mother. It seemed that Bettina Wells had played a fairly important role in preparing Grant's campaign for district attorney at the same time Jeri had worked in Senator Thomas Ryan's office. Nina found it hard not to believe there hadn't been any conflict of interests. She still suspected that Bettina might have fed facts to Jeri which were later used against Grant.

All this convinced her that as soon as she was on her feet again she would seek out Bettina and try and dig more facts from her. Now her brain began to get fuzzy as the drug started to work. She closed her eyes and in a matter of a few minutes descended into a deep sleep.

It was a sleep without dreams. She awoke to the sun streaming in through opened drapes and realized that she felt a great deal better. She raised herself in bed and timidly explored the injured area of her head. There was still a huge bump there but it did not feel so tender to the touch and most of the awful throbbing had subsided.

The door opened and Dr. Henry Taylor came in. The old doctor wore his usual smile. He said, "My, we're looking a lot better this morning."

She returned his smile. "And feeling better. Can I leave now?"

"Without breakfast? My wife is a fine cook!"

Nina laughed. "After breakfast, then!"

Dr. Taylor came over to her bedside and examined her. Then he said, "I'd like you to remain here until late afternoon. If you're still feeling all right you can go back to Blue Gables in time for dinner."

"Not before then?"

"I'd feel better if you had another half-day's bed rest here," the old doctor said. "I'll tell my wife to come in and get your order and you can enjoy the invalid's luxury of breakfast in bed."

Nina knew she had better go along with his wishes. The old doctor was friendly but firm in his demands. His wife prepared her a wonderful breakfast which included fresh strawberries and cream. Nina decided that being ill in this particular hospital was not an unpleasant experience.

Following the doctor's advice she closed her eyes and rested. He had advised against reading for a day or two. Some time passed and then the doctor's wife came into the room again.

"You have a visitor," the middle-aged woman said.

"Oh?"

The doctor's wife smiled. "Captain Zachary Miller. Shall I let him in?"

"Please do," she said. "I can think of no one I'd enjoy passing the time with more."

"I warn you, he's a talker," said the doctor's wife as she went out to get the old man.

She arranged the pillows behind her to make sitting up easier. The door opened and the old man came in hesitantly, his blue, peaked cap in hand. He looked like the relic of another, distant age in his faded blue suit with its golden buttons.

"How nice of you to visit me, Captain," she exclaimed.

The old man's wizened face showed a pleased smile. "I sort of reckoned you'd still be here," he said, standing awkwardly at the foot of her bed. "That was a right bad smash-up."

"I guess so," she said. "Please sit down."

"Thanks," he said, and found a plain chair which he drew up by her bed. "It so happened I was right at the scene when your car and that other one met."

"Were you driving?"

"Not in that fog," the old man said grimly. "I was standing by the crossroads waiting for the traffic to ease before crossing to walk back to my place. And I saw the big car sort of switch over to the wrong side of the road and make straight for you. I didn't know you were in the small car. But I sure knew there had to be a bad head-on collision!"

"And there was!" she said.

"Yep. Made a lot of noise," Captain Zachary Miller said with the complacence of an elderly bystander.

"I can imagine. I didn't know anything about it. I was out of it from the moment of the crash."

"Not much wonder," the Captain said. "The big fella in

the other car, he was all het up. I thought he was goin' to have a fit before Doc Taylor got there."

"I know him," she said. "He's a friend, also a guest at the Carters."

"Is that so?" the Captain seemed mildly interested.

"Yes. His name is Mort Venn."

"I have to say he's not much of a driver," Captain Zachary Miller told her. "Even taking the fog into consideration he should have done better than he did. He headed that car across the road and directly at you."

"I'm sure the fog blinded him. And he's not familiar with the road."

"But the road was straight enough there," the old man said with a frown on his stern old face. "I still say he could have avoided that accident if he hadn't lost his head."

Nina said, "Well, I guess it was meant to be. The main thing is that I wasn't hurt."

"But you could have been," the old man persisted. "I'd say it's a miracle you're alive and sitting up right now."

"I'm grateful for that," she said. "And I promise you I won't ever drive in thick island fog again. Greg said he wouldn't have allowed either of us to go out in cars if he'd been at home."

Captain Zachary Miller gave her a questioning glance. "You and Greg Carter engaged?"

"No," she said, smiling. "I was engaged to his brother Grant. But Greg and I are old friends."

The veteran captain nodded. "Grant was the one! I knew them both as boys."

"You said that."

"Yep. Greg was the mean one and Grant was always a nice young lad. They looked a lot alike, but they weren't alike. Not by a long shot."

"I found out the same thing when they were older," she agreed.

"I reckon you might have," the old captain said. "That Greg was always playing mean tricks on his brother."

"Grant wasn't like that."

"No. He put up with Greg's tricks and said nothing," Captain Zachary Miller said. "But it made me mad."

"I think Greg always remained jealous of Grant," she said.

"No doubt. Now Grant is dead and he has the whole thing to himself. Expect he'll get all his Aunt Madge's money," Captain Zachary Miller volunteered.

"Is she so wealthy?"

"Got scads of money," the old man said. "She comes from an island family that made their fortune in the whaling days. Those were the days when this island really had wealth. All the big mansions like Blue Gables date back to those times."

"I hadn't thought of that."

"It's true," the old Captain said. "When Madge Carter dies she'll leave plenty."

"I'm not sure that Greg needs it. He seems to have a very good business in Boston."

"Bet he spends plenty of money," Captain Miller said. "He'll be able to use some extra. Too bad that Grant got mixed up in politics. That was the end of him."

"I'm afraid it was."

"I didn't believe all that newspaper scandal about him. If it had been Greg I might have thought it true but not about Grant. I knew that boy too well. And who was that blonde gal who was supposed to be in the trouble with him?"

"Elise Venn," she said. "She was the wife of the man whose car ran into mine."

The old captain whistled. "What do you know! And his wife killed herself, didn't she?"

"That's what they said."

His shrewd old eyes fixed on her, "You don't sound like you believe it."

"I'm not sure I do."

"Oh?"

She said, "I think she may have fallen accidentally. She was drunk when it happened."

"But nobody knows the truth?"

"No. Her husband was in another room of the apartment when it happened. There were no other witnesses."

The Captain nodded grimly. "That means it stays a mystery. Anybody's guess."

"Yes. And the newspapers guessed suicide."

"They probably did that to make it look worse for Grant," he said.

"I have no doubt of that."

"Well, it's too bad," Captain Zachary Miller said. And then with true Yankee candor, he added, "If I were you I wouldn't settle for Greg as second choice."

She blushed. "Thanks for the advice. I really hadn't been thinking about it."

"I know every girl wants to get married," the old man said. "But I think some of them settles for too little. That could be your problem if you married Greg. He was a mean little boy and I think he might be a mean man."

"It's a good thing to remember," she said.

The Captain gave her another frank glance. "If you're looking for husband material you could do a lot worse than Derek Mills."

Startled by his directness, she said, "Derek Mills already has a wife."

"That's so. But she isn't well."

"Is she all that ill?"

"Folks on the island say so. She's had a couple of mental breakdowns. This time they say she isn't likely to come back. I reckon a good-looking young fellow like Derek will get a divorce if his wife lives on. But they say she's not in good physical health either and he might soon be a widower."

"He's very nice and it's a sad plight for him to be in," she sympathized.

The Captain nodded. "Yep. Last year he had a kind of love affair with a hippie girl who was up at the monastery for a while with a lot of other hippies. But I guess that's over."

She smiled at the old man. "There's not much about this island and its people you don't know."

"I hear a lot," he agreed.

"And you get around a good deal, too," she said.

He smiled proudly. "I'm driving a car these days. Did you know that?"

"No."

"Yep. It's not the latest model and it hasn't much pep but it suits me fine. I came over here in it today and anytime you want a drive just let me know."

"I may need a chauffeur occasionally now that my own car is wrecked," she told him.

"Well, just remember me," he said, rising. "Now I better go before the doc's wife puts me out."

"She wouldn't do that," Nina laughed.

"Don't be too sure about that," the old man said. He halted self-consciously by the door. "Well, I hope you get better soon."

"I expect to," she said. "I may leave the hospital this afternoon."

"Let me know if you need any help," Captain Zachary Miller said. "You can always get me at my place."

"I'll remember," she promised.

She felt good after the old man left. He was such a friendly, sensible old soul you couldn't help but enjoy his company. She also had been impressed by his comments about Greg. It was evident he distrusted the remaining Carter. His preference had been for Grant and he'd not hidden this from her. She knew that his accusations against Greg were probably justified no matter what sort of suave front Greg offered today. It was all too likely only a facade for the same mean young man who had so often cheated his brother.

Dr. Henry Taylor checked with her later in the afternoon and reluctantly allowed her to leave the hospital. He gave her a number of instructions for taking care of herself and then phoned Greg to come for her.

Nina was dressed and ready by the time Greg arrived. She settled her bill with the old doctor and thanked him. Then she went out and got in Greg's car.

He gave her a relieved glance as he started the engine. "I'm glad to get you out of that place."

"It wasn't bad at all," she told him.

"I know," he said, as they drove out of the hospital yard. "But it's just the thought of your being in a hospital which upset me. I don't know how to think of you as injured or ill. You've always been so active."

"The accident changed that. Dr. Taylor says I'll have to take it easy for a while."

As Greg drove his handsome face showed a frown. "There was something strange about that accident."

She glanced at him. "Why do you say that?"

"Mort doesn't seem to understand what made him switch to your side of the road. He still finds it hard to believe that it happened."

"I don't," she said.

He gave her a troubled glance. "Don't think I'm talking lightly. Mort says he had his headlights on but at the moment of the accident something seemed to overtake him. He was bewildered and couldn't see."

"Blame it on the fog."

Greg said, "He worries that it was something more than that."

"Had he been drinking?"

"No. But he thinks there was a spell cast over him."

She gasped. "A spell?"

"Don't think I'm talking nonsense," Greg warned her. "There may be truth in this speculation."

"Go on."

"Aunt Madge may not be as mad as we sometimes take her to be," the young man at the wheel said earnestly. "She has the opinion that Val Cramer and Jeri, and that Bettina woman, are all playing some sort of black magic game."

"There's no sense in that."

"I wonder," he said. "Aunt Madge isn't always that wrong. She is of the opinion that the people who bought the studio and barn are dealing in witchcraft!"

"What about Jeri Cramer?" she asked. "You brought her to the hospital with you when you came to see me."

Greg gave her a troubled side-glance. "The girl forced me to bring her to see you. She kept after me. I didn't want her with me but she insisted. It was almost as if she had to see how you'd come out of the accident for her own reasons."

Chapter Seven

Nina was shocked. "For her own reasons?"

"Yes."

"What could they be?"

He was looking straight ahead again as they drove along the main road. "I don't know. Unless Aunt Madge is right and those three are practicing some kind of witchcraft."

"That's medieval!" she protested.

"I just wonder," Greg said with a scowl. "A lot of strange things have happened since they've moved to that cottage. Aunt Madge should never have sold them the property."

"Too late to worry about that now," she said, rather amazed that the young man beside her should hold such views about the Cramers and Bettina.

He went on, "You know that Val makes those effigies. Heaven only knows what for! I think hardly anyone buys them. He must do it for some reason."

"Go on."

"Aunt Madge has a theory that he manipulates the effigies as some people manipulate puppets. Thus through his black magic he is able to effect the lives of the people whose likenesses he holds."

"There's a lot of Aunt Madge in all this," she chided him.

"Maybe so. But after what has happened I'm beginning to be worried. Elise meets a strange death. Then Grant is killed.

And now you are the victim of a freak accident."

"It was a foggy day."

"Mort thinks the fog had little to do with it. He feels he may have been placed under some sort of spell by Val Cramer. And maybe you were under his power as well."

She gave a small incredulous laugh. "That doesn't sound like the Mort I've talked to. He refuses to believe in the supernatural. He's told me so."

Greg's handsome face showed a hint of guilt. He said, "Well, let me tell you the accident has changed him."

"It must have!"

"I mean it," he said.

"Go on," she urged, not ready to believe him but wanting to hear what he had to say.

"He's badly shaken up. He has this idea he may have been used as an instrument to kill you. And this has made him think back and wonder about Elise and Grant."

"Both violent deaths and likely accidents in both cases since I don't see Elise as a suicide."

"Mort is wondering now."

"So Aunt Madge's superstitious fancies have been given a new life," she said in a cynical tone. "I wish I could agree with your theory but I don't think I can."

Greg said, "I don't blame you for being skeptical. But suppose this fellow Cramer has effigies of us all over at the studio and he's bending over some of us right now, telling us what we must do. Working his spell over us."

She stared at him. "You really think that possible?"

"I only know that Jeri was very anxious to visit you in the hospital. And no matter what she may say about her husband she is very devoted to him and does whatever he tells her to do."

"You're saying that she has been enticed into being an

accomplice to his black magic?"

"I think it's possible," he said as he brought the car to a halt before the front entrance of Blue Gables. "She might even be under hypnosis."

Nina shook her head. "It's all very far-fetched."

He said, "I can't help what you think. I just wanted to bring you up to date." And he got out, opened the car door for her and saw her into the old mansion.

The first person they met was Kay Dunninger. The dark-haired secretary looked pleased to see her and said, "I'm so glad you're back and that the accident wasn't more serious."

She smiled ruefully. "From my standpoint it was serious enough. My car is a total wreck."

Kay said, "Just so long as you're all right."

Greg stood there looking uncomfortable and asked her, "Do you think you should go up to your room and rest?"

"Yes," she said. "I should. I promised Dr. Taylor I'd take it easy for a while and I'm sure he'll be around checking on me."

"Do you want Kay to see you upstairs?" Greg asked, a worried look on his tanned face.

"Of course not," she protested with a smile. "I'm not all that much an invalid. I feel fine except that my head is a little light."

She left the two in the reception hall and made her way up to her bedroom. She felt somewhat giddy and realized that she'd been in worse condition than she'd thought. The strain of leaving the hospital and driving home had wearied her. She stretched out on the bed, closed her eyes and dropped off to sleep.

When she opened her eyes sometime later she was not alone in the bedroom. Aunt Madge Carter was standing at the foot of the bed staring at her. The familiar, flabby white face under the hennaed hair was set in anxious lines. The pale blue eyes were fixed on her in a troubled fashion.

"When I came in you were sleeping so quietly I worried that you might have died," the old woman said.

She raised herself on an elbow. "Nothing like that."

Madge Carter studied her. "You're pale. You don't look well!"

"I had a serious head injury," she said. "I'm lucky that I'm not in worse shape."

The old woman's thin lips trembled. "I know everyone here thinks I'm a silly old woman, but I had a premonition something like this was going to happen."

Sitting up on the edge of the bed, she asked, "Why do you say that?"

Aunt Madge's thin hands were clasped together in front of her and now she began to twist them nervously. "I knew it because of what had gone on before and because of seeing the ghost of Elise."

"Oh?"

The old woman nodded solemnly. "Yes. I saw her again. The night of the fog—the night you had your accident! She was standing in the lower hall gazing up the stairway. I was on the landing and I became so frightened I ran back to my bedroom and didn't leave it for the rest of the night."

Nina was concerned by the old woman's account of seeing the blonde ghost again. She said, "You're sure you saw her? It wasn't just a case of imagination?"

"I saw her," Madge Carter said with dignity. "Don't suggest I'm daft. I'm as sane as anyone under this roof."

"I'm sure you are," she said.

The old woman went on in frightened fashion, "I think it has something to do with him."

"Him?"

"That artist—Val Cramer! There's been nothing but trouble here since I sold them that property. I made a bad mistake!"

Nina said, "I really don't think so."

"I'm certain of it," Madge Carter insisted. "That man works spells! And that mother-in-law of his, that Bettina, is a weird one."

"You oughtn't to allow yourself to hold such ideas," Nina reproved her. "I don't think you're being fair, and I'm sure you'd find your theories very difficult to prove."

The old woman looked bleak. "You won't listen to me now. But maybe you'll be glad to later. More things will happen—you wait and see!"

The wizened old autocrat left her after this dour pronouncement. Greg had been right about the opinions held by the others in the old house. Nina found it easy to understand why they should be upset but she felt the sinister happenings had some different source. It was surely unfair to blame an auto crash caused by the dense fog on Val Cramer. In spite of her assertions to the contrary, Nina felt that the elderly Madge Carter was suffering from delusions.

Nina rested awhile longer and then went down to dinner. Mort Venn was at the table and in a contrite mood. When the meal was over he accompanied her to the living room and tried to apologize for what had happened.

The big, moon-faced man said, "I'll never forgive myself for running into your car."

"It was the fog," she said.

"That still doesn't satisfy me," the big man said soberly. "I should have seen your car in time to avoid the crash."

"It's over with, forget about it."

"You could have been killed."

"I wasn't."

The eyes behind his horn-rimmed glasses revealed his distress. He said, "That's no credit to me. I seemed to go blank for a moment. As if someone had placed me under a spell."

"Probably tension."

"No," he argued. "It was more than that. I'm sure of it. After the accident I was still in a sort of daze."

"You were probably stunned. That was to be expected."

"I think I was used as a puppet by Val Cramer," the big man told her.

She shook her head. "I've heard about that. I don't believe it."

"Something strange happened," Mort insisted.

She gave him a soft pat on the arm. "Don't worry about it anymore. You're exaggerating it out of all proportions. And I don't want that."

The big man looked at her wryly. "Now you have an idea how I feel about your delving into the past and dragging up things about Grant and Elise. I see that as just as big a mistake as you do about my suspecting Cramer."

"That's different," Nina protested.

"I don't think so."

"I'm trying to establish facts about happenings in the past. I'm not attempting to prove there was witchcraft or anything like that involved."

His face was grim. "Yet you believe you saw the ghost of my wife."

She knew he had her on this point. She sighed and turned away from him. "I did see what seemed to be a phantom Elise," she admitted.

He followed her. "You ask me to believe that and yet you refuse to listen to my theories."

Nina glanced at him. "I think they are too wild. I can well

believe that Bettina or Jeri may have had some part in building the scandalous case against Grant and Elise. But I don't see them as dabblers in witchcraft."

"We differ in that," he said.

She sat down in a nearby easy chair and glanced up at him. "I've been thinking about that land deal Grant and Elise were said to have managed. Where would your wife have gotten the money for buying that land?"

"Not from me," he said.

"Where?"

"I don't know."

"Had she any money of her own?"

"Not any amount," Mort Venn said with a frown. "At least not that I knew of. But Grant could have found the money for her. He had plenty of it."

"I suppose so," she agreed.

"The fact is that, aside from the money having been paid for the land, we don't know anything else," Mort said grimly. "The letters sent anonymously to the newspapers only gave part of the story. We're in the dark about a good deal."

"About too much," she said.

"I agree," Mort said. "But we do know the land was bought in an underhand way and a big profit made on it when the state took it over and found Grant's name on certain of the deeds, Elise's on others."

"I'm sure Senator Ryan connived it somehow," she said.

"How?" Mort asked her.

"I don't know," she confessed.

"That's where it always ends," the big man said. "Your best bet is to forget about it and marry Greg."

She gave him a grim smile. "Thanks for the advice."

"I mean it," Mort said earnestly. And in a lower, more confidential tone he leaned over to add, "I guess you must have noticed that Kay Dunninger is making a great play for him. And as his new secretary she has some advantages."

"I'm not interested."

"You should be," Mort said.

They talked a few minutes more and then she went up to bed. She was somewhat startled by the big man's sudden acceptance of Aunt Madge Carter's weird theories that Val Cramer was practicing witchcraft. The idea that the artist was influencing them all and arranging dark fates for them was not one she would have expected Mort to embrace. She could only put his belief down to his honest guilt about the accident.

Before turning out the bedroom lights she glanced out the window at the gardens and the lights of Dark Harbor in the distance. There was no hint of a ghost in the garden tonight, but she still had eerie feelings about the old house and its grounds. She knew she would continue to have them until she solved the mystery of it all. And she wondered if that would be possible.

This island thirty miles from the mainland was a haunted sort of place, cut off from the real world it seemed, especially when the fog enveloped it. She wished that she could leave at once, but she knew that she couldn't until she had made a few more attempts to clear the name of Grant Carter, the man she still loved.

Turning away from the window with a wistful look on her lovely face she thought of Mort Venn's rather clumsy attempts to make her shift her affections to Greg. She knew deep in her heart that this wasn't possible. It would be easier for her to fall in love with someone like Derek Mills.

This brought her to thinking about her weird experience in the pool the other night, of seeing Greg's face so clearly in the shadows and then being drawn under the water. Greg had not been on the island that night, or so he claimed. And the fact he'd made the journey back the next morning on the ferry seemed to bear his story out. So who had she seen?

Derek Mills had suggested she'd either allowed her imagination to construct the face out of the shadows or that she'd seen the ghost of Grant. This last was a frightening possibility which she'd never seriously considered before. Now she knew that she must think about it.

With this disturbing thought she got into bed and turned out the lights. Through the open window she could hear the distant sound of the waves washing against the shore. She fell asleep lulled by the steady rhythm of the breakers. But it was an uneasy sleep filled with visions of Grant returned from his watery grave. She found herself walking in the gardens only to be confronted by the vision of a sad-faced and dripping Grant, as if he'd walked out of the ocean and come there to haunt her.

She screamed at the sight of the spectre and ran from him. Sobbing in her flight she became lost in a weird, shadowy world which was completely foreign to her. She kept seeking escape from this dark place of forbidding forests and huge gray boulders which blocked her way at every step. At last she found a clear channel through the eerie blackness and came out in the open only to be faced by the tall, Lincolnesque figure of Val Cramer. The artist wore a malevolent smile and reached out to grasp her in his powerful hands.

It was at this point that she wakened. It was already dawn and she stared up into the grayness of her bedroom still trembling from the ordeal of her nightmare. In the distance she heard the mournful crying of a night bird and she tried to make some sense of the strange nightmare she'd had. But it was too disconnected. Slowly sleep came back to her and she slept quietly until morning.

Shortly after breakfast she had a visitor. It was Dr. Henry Taylor. She led the old man into the sewing room which was deserted and he talked to her about her condition.

"Are you feeling better?" the old doctor wanted to know as they sat in wicker chairs opposite each other.

"Yes," she said. "Most of the dizziness has left me."

"A good sign."

She frowned slightly. "But I'm terribly nervous. And I'm having bad nightmares."

The white-haired man arched an eyebrow. "Well, I can give you tablets to see that you sleep soundly."

"A drugged sleep?"

"I suppose you could call it that. I had a strong sedative in mind."

"I'd rather not take anything," she protested.

His lined face showed mild surprise. "Then you prefer the nightmares?"

"Yes. To taking a drug which would send me into an unnatural sleep," she said. "I'm afraid of what might happen to me if I were too drugged to be aware of what might be going on around me."

Dr. Taylor showed interest. "You mean you are afraid of this old house?"

"Yes."

"I see," he said. "Well, I suppose there shouldn't be much mystery to that. It hasn't a happy history."

"I wouldn't remain here or on the island for a moment if I weren't here for a purpose," she told him.

"You don't like our island?"

"It's not a matter of liking or disliking," she said. "It has too many unhappy associations for me. I first came here with Grant."

"So you told me."

"But that's not important to you," she said with a wry smile. "You've come here to see how I've recovered from the accident. I'd say my recovery is almost complete."

The old doctor said, "I wouldn't be too quick to agree to that. You've admitted that your nerves are still edgy, the dreams are part of that. And let me warn you that you may react more strongly to events around you than you would otherwise. One doesn't recover from shock in a few days. So try to understand that your reactions may be heightened unduly for a little. It could save you from needless fears."

"Thank you," she said. "You've been very kind to me."

"You had a close call with death," the old doctor told her soberly. "I feel it's important to keep a close watch on you."

After he left she went out on the patio which ran the full length of the old mansion. Mort Venn was seated there in slacks and dark sports shirt open at the neck. He wore dark glasses and had the morning paper in his hands.

Putting the paper on the table beside him, he said, "You had an early visit from the doctor."

"Yes," she said, taking the chair across the table from him. "He's still worried about me."

"So am I."

"But I'm perfectly all right."

Mort looked at her bleakly. "I can't forget that you might have been killed as a result of my negligence."

"You're blaming yourself when you should blame the fog."

"I bear a good part of the responsibility," the big man said. "What about the replacement of your car? My insurance will look after it."

"There's no dealer on the island. I'll have to wait until I return to Boston," she said.

"Do you want me to rent a car for you?"

"No. I don't need one that badly. I can borrow yours or even Greg's if I want to drive somewhere."

Mort's round face showed concern. "It doesn't seem fair that you should be restricted this way."

"I'm just as happy without a car," she told him. "Don't worry about it."

He said, "Greg is out in his boat. If the weather is good tonight he suggested we all go for a midnight cruise around the island."

"It sounds like fun," she said.

"I think it could be," the big man agreed.

"Greg gets great enjoyment from his boat," she said.

"It's the thing which seems to interest him most," Mort agreed with a sigh. "I'm getting restless. I ought to leave here tomorrow."

"Why?"

"Just a feeling," he said. "And I do have a business to look after, you know."

"You have a competent staff to do most of the work, don't you?"

"Yes," he agreed. "But there are certain decisions no one but me can make. When Elise was alive it was different. We shared the main responsibilities."

Nina studied the face of the big man. "You must miss her a great deal."

"I do," he said, frowning slightly. "But I'm trying to be a little more sensible than you in my loss. I know I can't bring her back and I try to adjust to that. You would do well to remember that about Grant. He's dead and you can't change it."

"I don't expect to change it," she said firmly. "I'm only trying to straighten out the record of his past. Clear his name of all the evil things that have been said about him."

"No one but you cares."

"Then it's enough that I care," she said.

He shook his head in despair. "You are a stubborn little creature. You won't listen to good advice."

"Not in this case," she said. "I'm sure both Grant and Elise are unhappy in death. That is why their ghosts haunt this place."

The man with the dark glasses gazed at her grimly. "No one has seen them but you."

"I won't argue about that."

Mort hunched in his chair. "In my opinion if there is any strange business going on here we can put it down to that Val Cramer and his weird kind of art experiments. I think he and the rest of them over there are dabbling in witchcraft."

"You didn't used to think that."

"I do now," he said. "If there are things going on which can't be explained, I say chalk them up to that trio over there."

Nina evaded offering an opinion by saying, "I'm not too sure about anything anymore."

After lunch she experienced a strange restlessness. She found her mood difficult to understand. And to try and rid herself of it she decided to walk across the broad lawns to the cottage occupied by the Cramers and Bettina. It was almost as if some inner voice were directing her to make a visit there.

As she crossed the broad grassy expanse the sun temporarily went behind clouds to give the day a sudden touch of gloom. She gazed at the cottage ahead and the barn studio beside it and wondered if she'd find any of the group at home. She hoped there would be someone there besides Val Cramer. The artist made her nervous and she didn't relish the prospect of a visit alone with him.

With this in mind she headed directly toward the cottage entrance. The door of the white Cape Cod style building was painted a bright yellow with matching window trim. She went to the door and used the black iron knocker to announce her presence.

After a short wait the door was opened by Bettina Wells. The blonde woman looked mildly surprised at seeing her. She said, "Nina! I didn't know you're recovered so quickly."

"I'm feeling fine again," she said. "I hope you don't mind my intruding on you."

"I'm glad to see you," the older woman said with a smile. "Do come in!"

"Thank you," Nina said. "I became very restless and felt I had to get away from Blue Gables for a little."

"I can understand," Bettina sympathized as she showed her into a living room with the shutters closed to keep out the sun. The room was in semi-darkness as a result and Nina was not able to make out much about its furnishings.

She sat on a divan and Bettina sat in an easy chair near her. The older woman asked her, "Would you care for a drink?"

"No, thanks," she said. "I just wanted to walk a little and talk to someone."

"I see," Bettina said, gazing at her across the shadowed room. "You came close to being killed, didn't you?"

"Yes. It was a nasty accident."

"The fog is so thick when it really comes in," Bettina said. "I suppose Mort feels badly about it."

"He blames himself and that is wrong."

"That is like Mort," Bettina agreed.

"Where is Jeri?" Nina asked by way of changing the subject.

"She and Val have gone to Dark Harbor for some things. She waits until she is completely out of supplies and then they shop."

Nina laughed lightly. "The artistic temperament."

"Not entirely," the blonde woman said. "I blame it on Jeri. And she is not an artist. Just rather impractical."

"And you're not."

"No, I have a definite system for doing things. I suppose it is part of my business training. I like order. Jeri couldn't care less."

"Then she and Val should get along well together," Nina suggested.

"They do. I only worry that she is too much a slave to him. She sees everything through his eyes. He didn't want her to go on having a career of her own and so she has given up law. I think that is a shame."

"It is. Especially if she had talent."

"She did have," Bettina said. "But it does no good for me to preach to her. She no longer listens. Val controls her thoughts these days."

Nina listened to this with renewed interest. It seemed to bear out the theory that Val Cramer had his wife under an almost hypnotic influence. And this naturally led to the other concern that he might also have some sinister method of influencing those whose effigies he had fashioned.

She said, "Then Val is a very strong personality."

"Very strong," Bettina agreed.

She said, "Is he still constructing those effigies?"

"Yes. It's his main interest these days," Bettina said. She gave her an odd, searching stare. "Don't you think they are most unusual?"

"They are unusual," she said carefully.

"He pours his very soul into those figures," the older woman said.

"Do you consider that healthy?" she asked.

There was a short silence before Bettina replied. Then she said, "I suppose it depends on one's viewpoint."

Nina thought this a rather evasive answer. She said, "I've been meaning to have a talk with you. That is one of my reasons for coming here."

"Oh?" Bettina sounded almost apprehensive.

"Yes," she went on. "I know that you worked for Mort when he and Elise were running Grant's political campaign."

"So?"

"It seemed to me that you must have known most of what was going on," she said. "And I wondered if you might perhaps remember something of those days that would help me."

"Help you in what?"

"In trying to clear Grant's name of all the scandal."

Bettina looked uneasy. She said, "I really had a very minor position with the agency. I didn't know any of the inner workings there."

"But you must have had many contacts with Grant and Elise," she pressed the woman.

"I saw them almost every day during the campaign but in a most casual way."

"Did it strike you that Grant and Elise could be having an affair?"

"That never crossed my mind," Bettina protested.

"There was plenty of talk about it. Didn't that cause some interest in the office?"

"We put it down to dirty campaigning on the opposition's part," the blonde woman said rather lamely.

"So you saw nothing in the actions of Grant or Elise to make you think the story was true?"

"No. But I can't offer myself as an authority."

"You were there," she said. "And surely you must have felt someone was responsible for the stories. Perhaps someone who was pretending to be Grant's friend. One of his workers."

"I never thought about it," Bettina said, sounding strangely flustered.

Nina went on sternly, "I wish you would give it some thought. I think there were leaks to the enemy camp. Facts were supplied to Senator Ryan and his supporters which were conveniently twisted to make up the smear stories. Grant and Elise were friends, no one doubts that. But in the smear campaign they were made to seem lovers with a guilty secret. The business of the land transactions had to be the work of someone else."

"It was done in their names," Bettina reminded her.

"I still don't believe it."

"And you don't believe Elise took her life because the truth came out?" the older woman asked.

"No. I think she was drinking because she was badly upset and her death came about as an accident."

"I see."

"Jeri was in Ryan's office," Nina went on. "Even if she were in a different department I'd think that some information must have seeped through to her."

"She says not."

"I think she may have forgotten," Nina said. "But I'm sure she must have heard some things. Just as you may be overlooking some important events. Memory can be tricky."

Bettina said, "I'll think about it. I'll try to remember anything I feel may be of help to you."

"I hope you will."

The older woman stared at her through the shadows of the living room. "What about Mort Venn? He should know more than anyone else. Why don't you question him?"

"I have."

"And?"

"I can't say that he has been all that helpful," she told the blonde woman. "He is very confused and tortured about the entire affair. He loved Elise and Grant was his friend, so he found it hard to believe the tales about them even at the time they first appeared."

"Surely he can look at it in retrospect now?"

Nina shook her head. "Unfortunately that doesn't seem to be the case. He's still hopelessly muddled as to what he believes. And this makes him an unreliable witness."

"That is too bad."

"I couldn't agree more," Nina said.

"There may be another way to solve the mystery," the older woman said.

"How?"

"My crystal," Bettina said. "I have a most valuable crystal ball which I use in séances from time to time. We could try calling on the spirits of Elise and Grant. See if they will tell us the truth."

A chill shot down Nina's spine at the thought. "No," she said. "I'd prefer to base my work on whatever you and Jeri can remember."

"I think you are making a mistake," the older woman said. "A séance might settle everything. We could have you and Mort and anyone else close to Grant and Elise join us at the table. I seldom fail to get a message from the other side."

"Not for a while at least," she said, rising. The suggestion had made her nervous. She had a strong desire to escape the dark living room. "I must walk back to Blue Gables now."

Bettina also got up. "I'll go with you. I'd enjoy a walk in the air. I'll have to stop by the studio first and leave a message for Val and Jeri as to where I've gone."

They left the cottage and went across to the gray barn studio. Bettina unlocked the door and they went inside along the dark, curtained corridor. Nina glanced uneasily around her but saw the effigies which had reclined in the alcoves before had been removed.

She followed Bettina into the artist's workshop and while the older woman picked up a pad to leave a message, she strolled over to the bench to see what Val might be working on. She was at once interested in an item covered with an upturned woven basket. She could see that there was a sculpted head beneath it and assumed that it was a carving on which the artist was presently engaged.

On impulse she lifted the basket to inspect the head and what she saw sent a cold wave of terror through her. She was staring at a partially-completed carving of her own head.

Chapter Eight

There was a sharp gasp from Bettina and the blonde woman came up to her. She said, "You weren't supposed to see that!"

Still stunned Nina looked up from the wood carving of her face and head. "Wasn't I?"

"No," the older woman said, obviously upset. And she hastily placed the upturned basket over the carving again.

She stared at Bettina. "Why is he making a carving of me?"

Bettina's smile was not very convincing as she answered, "He planned to surprise you."

"He managed that," Nina said, gradually recovering from her shock and now beginning to feel some anger. "But I gave him no permission to make such a carving."

"Of course you didn't. But he wouldn't expect that he'd need it."

"I didn't model for him."

"He has a clever memory for detail. He's met you a few times. That is all he requires."

She stared at the basket-covered carving again and with a distinct feeling of fear said, "I'm not interested in becoming one of his effigies."

"You mustn't tell him that!" Bettina said placatingly. "You would be bound to hurt his feelings, and Jeri would feel badly as well."

"I don't care," she said. "I'd prefer that he didn't go on with it."

"Why?"

She gazed into the questioning countenance of the older woman and hesitated. She didn't dare to say outright that she believed the artist exerted spells over the subjects of his expert imagery.

At last she said lamely, "I don't consider myself that interesting a subject. He should spend his time on more important people."

The blonde woman smiled in a rather strange, knowing manner. "Why not let Val decide that?"

"I'm not pleased about it."

"Don't say anything yet," Bettina counselled her. "Wait until he has finished the project and then I'm sure you'll approve."

Nina saw there was to be no arguing with the woman. Bettina would not be swayed, so for the moment it would be best to drop the matter. Yet her discovery had frightened her and she meant to talk to Greg and Mort about it at the first opportunity. She would also mention it to Derek Mills when she saw him again. It suddenly occurred to her that she hadn't seen the handsome museum director since before her accident.

The older woman broke into her reverie, saying, "I've left a note for Val and Jeri. Now we can be on our way."

She made no protest since she was anxious to leave the depressing atmosphere of the studio. But as she emerged in the sunlight again she couldn't remove from her mind the picture of that still unfinished carving of her head resting on the artist's workbench. They began strolling toward Blue Gables and Bettina talked on while Nina scarcely heard anything the older woman was saying.

Aunt Madge Carter was seated in a chair on the patio. When she saw Bettina with Nina, a grim look settled on her ancient, flabby face. The matriarch of Blue Gables did not approve of Mrs. Wells.

Ignoring the blonde woman she at once addressed herself to Nina, saying, "You had a phone call while you were out."

"Did I?" she asked.

"Yes," the old woman said severely. "That Derek Mills at the Museum. He wants you to call him back."

"I will," she said.

"I can't imagine what he wants," Madge Carter went on. "He rarely comes to see us anymore."

Nina said, "He came to the cocktail party."

"There were so many here that day I lost count," the old woman said. Then she glanced at Bettina Wells. "Are you spending the summer on the island?" she asked.

Bettina seemed not at all put out by the old woman's manner. She said, "Yes. I think we probably shall. Val keeps his studio open three afternoons and evenings a week, occasionally more often. He's doing very well. It will pay him to stay the entire season."

The old woman eyed her wrathfully. "Is he still making those ghastly figures?"

"His effigies?" Bettina said with an amused look. "Yes. That is his chief occupation. The smaller things he carves for the tourist trade are just a sideline."

"I don't like it," Madge Carter declared. "I wish he'd destroy the ones he made of Grant and that Venn woman."

"Destroy them?" Val's mother-in-law exclaimed in surprise. "But they are works of art!"

"If I'd known that was the sort of art he was going to be doing I wouldn't have sold you the property," the old woman informed her.

"I'm sorry you don't approve," Bettina said. "He is a fine artist."

"Everyone is entitled to his opinion," Madge Carter said in a tone of total disapproval.

It was an awkward situation, but Bettina solved it by turning to Nina and saying, "Now that I've seen you safely home I'll be on my way."

"Thank you," Nina said.

The blonde woman told her, "Watch yourself. You mustn't try to do too much yet." And to the old woman she said, "Good afternoon, Miss Carter. It is always pleasant having a chat with you."

Having said that the blonde woman turned and strode out across the lawn in the direction of the distant guesthouse.

From her chair, Madge Carter grumbled, "Upstart of a woman! I can't abide her!"

She turned to the old woman and said, "Then why did you sell her the cottage and barn?"

"I didn't know what she was like then," Aunt Madge declared indignantly. "We've had nothing but trouble since they came here! That artist and his weird figures, and her with that crystal ball! Modern witchcraft, that's what it is!"

Considering what she had seen and the discussion she'd had with Bettina, she felt in no mood to argue with the old woman. It could be that Madge Carter was all too correct in her opinions about the trio.

Anxious to get away from the discussion and Aunt Madge, she said, "I'd better go and make that phone call."

"I suppose you had," Aunt Madge said. "It came about an hour ago."

She went inside to the nearest phone in the hallway. The old mansion was cool and quiet. She sat by the phone table and opened the directory to look up the number of the museum in the dim light. Having found it, she dialed the number and asked the young woman who answered if she might speak with Derek Mills.

There was a slight wait before Derek's pleasant voice came on the line. "Yes?" he said.

"It's Nina Patton," she told him. "Miss Carter said you called me."

"So I did," he replied at once. "I left the island the morning after your accident and I didn't get a chance to call on you at the hospital."

"I realized that."

"Don't think it was lack of interest," he assured her. "I've been thinking about you constantly. I was going to wire flowers from the mainland but I decided I'd wait and get in touch with you as soon as I returned."

"I'm glad you did," she said.

"And you're really well again?"

"Yes."

"That's wonderful," Derek said. "I was very worried. You should never drive in that fog again."

"I promise I won't."

"How about our dinner date?" he asked.

"I'd like to see you," she said.

"What about tomorrow night?"

"Fine."

"Very well," he said. "I'll come by for you around seven. We can go to a very nice restaurant on the shore road. I think you'll like it."

"I'll look forward to it," she said.

They said their goodbyes and she put down the phone to see that Greg was standing in the doorway of the living room watching her. A slight flush came to her cheeks as she realized that he must have heard at least part of her conversation.

She rose and walked down the hallway to him. "I didn't know you were home," she said.

The good-looking Greg eyed her with slight annoyance. "Was that Derek Mills on the phone?"

"Yes. How did you know?"

"I heard you say Derek."

"Then it wasn't hard to guess," she said, trying to dismiss it lightly.

Greg was staring at her hard. "You're going out with him?"

"Yes. Why not?"

He shrugged. "No reason. It just strikes me as funny that you are interested in everyone but me."

"That isn't so!" she protested.

"I begin to think it."

"Nonsense."

He said, "You still hate me because of what happened to Grant. Because I look like him you resent me. You forget that we were the first to meet. You didn't know Grant until months later."

"Must we go over that again?" she asked wearily.

"I feel like someone on the outside," he complained. "I'm sure you wouldn't be here at all if you didn't have that obsession about trying to clear Grant's name."

"Probably not."

"At least you're honest in admitting it."

"I always try to be honest with you," she said.

Greg smiled grimly. "I wonder. I'm taking Mort and Kay out for an evening cruise in my boat. Will you join us?"

Ordinarily it wouldn't have been an invitation to interest her, but because of his bad mood she decided to humor him by accepting. She said, "Yes. I'll be glad to go along."

He looked pleased. "Great! We'll leave here about eight

and we'll be back before midnight. It should be nice with lots of stars overhead."

"How far are you going?"

"Around the harbor and then out along the shore at this end of the island," he said. "The water is as smooth as glass. You needn't worry about getting seasick."

"I never have," she told him. And then she went on to say, "I was over visiting Bettina this afternoon."

He showed interest. "Were you?"

"Yes. She was alone, Val and Jeri were in Dark Harbor on a shopping trip. We went across to the studio and I stumbled on something which bothered me."

"What?"

"I found a partially completed carving of my face on Val's workbench."

Greg frowned. "I'm not surprised. So he's adding you to his company of effigies. Better watch out!"

"It gave me an eerie feeling," she confessed.

"No wonder, after what has happened to most of the people whose likenesses he has over there! Did you give him permission to do it?"

"No."

"He has nerve," Greg said grimly. "You ought to tell him you don't want it completed."

"I told Bettina that, and she seemed to think it would be a mistake."

"Naturally. She's part of whatever deviltry he's up to!"

"But even if I did tell him that he could still finish my effigy without my knowing anything about it."

"I suppose that's so," Greg admitted. "But I don't like it."

"Neither do I," she said. "He's doing the carving from memory. He has a remarkable talent if you could only guess what use he is putting it to."

"I know," Greg agreed. "Better not mention this to Aunt Madge or she'll be having fits. She's certain that Val Cramer is some kind of warlock."

"I'll be careful," she said. "But I did want to tell you."

At dinner that night Aunt Madge held the spotlight. Mort asked her about the Unitarian Church whose tall bell tower dominated the island. And she at once launched into a history of the old church and its tower.

"It's a clock tower now," she told the group around the table, "but in the old days it was a watchtower for fires. There were no fire alarms so the bell was rung and the watchman up in the tower would wave a lantern in the direction of the fire."

The stout Mort said, "I'd say the bell has a fine quality."

"It ought to have," the old woman said proudly. "It was cast in Portugal, intended to be used there. But the order was canceled, and a Pirate Island captain who was looking for a bell for the church here bought it for five hundred dollars. Later a Boston church, impressed by the beauty of the bell's tone, offered us a handsome figure for it, but the offer was refused."

Mort asked the old woman more questions about the island and she answered them at length. It was clear that she enjoyed doing this and the meal went along well with everyone in a good humor. Nina forgot her fears of the afternoon and began to anticipate the projected cruise in Greg's pleasure boat. As soon as dinner was over she went upstairs, changed into a fairly heavy rose pants suit and took along a raincoat.

She met Kay Dunninger on the stairway and saw that the girl was wearing a white wool sweater over her linen dress. Nina said, "You're going prepared just as I am."

"I'm sure it will be cold out on the ocean," Kay said with

some worry as they continued on down the stairs.

"You don't sound enthusiastic about the evening."

"I'm not," Kay admitted. "I'm only going because Greg seemed so set on it."

"I know," she agreed. "I feel exactly the same way."

Greg was waiting for them in his station wagon. Mort and Kay sat in the back seat while she and Greg shared the front. They drove down through Dark Harbor past the many tourists wandering up and down the steep main street. As they passed the Gray Heron Inn, Greg pointed out the dour owner of the hotel and tavern standing in the doorway.

"That's Matthew Kimble," he told her. "He's a kind of mystery on the island. He was away for a couple of years and the story is that he spent them in prison. His mother operated the place until he came back. Most of his business is with tourists and the few fishermen who are friendly with him. A lot of the islanders won't go in there at all."

From the back seat Mort Venn asked, "Didn't Grant used to be friendly with him?"

A bitter look crossed Greg's face as he drove on down toward the wharves. "Yes," he said. "For some reason I've never been able to guess they got along well. Grant often stopped by there at night for a beer. Matt Kimble seemed to like him."

Nina recalled Grant's telling her about the tavern owner and saying that the dour man had many good qualities but was misunderstood by the islanders.

Aloud, she said, "I'm sure Grant spoke of him, but I've never been in there."

"It's not a fancy place," Greg said. "A workingman's bar and the hotel above isn't much."

They reached the wharves and drove along the cobblestone street which fronted on them until they came to a dock for pleasure craft. Greg parked the car near the wharf and they got out and walked across the gray wooden planks which had weathered countless storms. Steps led down to a marina-like structure where Greg's motor cruiser was moored.

Greg went ahead and he and Mort helped the girls aboard. Then Greg took control of the cruiser as Mort looked after casting off. Within a few minutes the motor of the big pleasure cruiser was humming and the sleek craft was nosing out into the open harbor, cutting the waves with its sharp prow and leaving a trail of white foam in its wake.

In the beginning she and Kay stood up front with the two men enjoying the view of the docks and the village as they moved away from the shore. They made the trip around the harbor and then slipped out through the rather narrow inlet which joined the harbor and the ocean beyond. As darkness came they were far out along the coast where the fishing vessels plied their trade. Greg had turned on the lights of the cruiser so that it could readily be seen and identified. And every so often they passed other craft with their red and green lights and spotlights.

It began to get really cold and Kay complained and left them to go into the cabin. Mort stayed with Greg at the wheel and Nina moved about the more than thirty feet of the cruiser. The stars were out in full majesty. She stared up at them in awe and felt that this sight alone justified the trip. She was also beginning to feel the night chill and tried walking back to the deserted stern of the craft to see if it might be warmer there.

The breeze was lighter but it was still cold. She stood there debating if she should join Kay in the forward cabin. As she pondered on this she gazed back at the shore of Pirate Island and saw the twinkling lights of scattered houses along its coast. All at once and for no particular reason she had an overwhelming sense of fear.

She stood there alone in the dark stern of the cruiser literally paralyzed with this sudden terror. It was as if some hidden instinct was sending out a warning. Alarmed by this strange fear she made up her mind to hurry back and join Mort and Greg. Summoning her small residue of courage she turned to start the walk back to the forward section of the craft where the others were when out of the shadows a ghost materialized. The ghost of Elise!

Nina screamed as the phantom with the long blonde hair came at her in menacing fashion. Before she could dodge away from the path of the oncoming phantom she was roughly shoved over the side into the cold waves.

She screamed again as she toppled back into the water. For a fleeting instant she had a glimpse of the blonde phantom peering down at her from the stern of the cruiser. Then she was alone in the chill ocean water with the cruiser rapidly vanishing into the night. She was an excellent swimmer and she at once began the struggle to survive.

The waves which had seemed so calm when she was on the cruiser seemed anything but that now. The cold water was numbing and she knew that it was merely a matter of time until she'd have to give up struggling and sink into a watery grave. Only her determination kept her battling to stay afloat.

The ghost of Elise had found its way to the cruiser and had deliberately attacked her. She tried to tell herself that the others would miss her and they would return in search of her. But even as she did so she knew that she was deceiving herself. It might be some time before she was missed and then they would have no idea where to search for her. In any case it wouldn't matter because by that time she'd be drowned!

Her will to battle the cold waves diminished. She began to

think how easy it would be to give up, to sink slowly below the surface of the waves and be at rest. Her swimming became less frantic and she barely managed to struggle on. Her energy was badly depleted when she thought she heard the sound of a ship's horn and sensed the throbbing of engines in the water near her.

At first she felt it was an illusion, a prelude to her giving up and sinking below the ocean's surface. But then she saw the red and green boat lights bobbing up and down against the darkness above her. And in the next moment a spotlight was switched on and swept across the area where she was struggling amid the waves.

The horn blasted again and she heard someone shouting. She tried to shout back but couldn't manage anything but a hoarse croaking. Next a buoy came hurtling through the air and dropped in the water near her. She gave a gasp of joy and began wearily making her way toward it. It eluded her on the first attempt and then she caught it the second time and held on to it grimly.

From the boat there came further reassuring shouts as the buoy was dragged in on a line. Within minutes she was being helped up into the boat by strong hands. She fell exhausted on the deck as her rescuers bent over her anxiously. From their voices and comments she guessed that she was on one of the many fishing vessels around the island.

Someone came hurrying back to her and the neck of a bottle was forced between her lips. She felt a quantity of burning liquid enter her mouth and go coursing down her throat. She began to feel that she was alive and might go on living.

"Fetch a blanket for her, Jim," a coarse male voice ordered someone.

She looked up into the grim face of an elderly man and in a

small voice said, "Thanks. I was sure I was going to drown."

"You would have if we hadn't spotted you out there," the elderly man said. "What happened? Were you in some pleasure craft that sank?"

"No. I fell overboard," she said. No use to talk of ghosts and being shoved into the sea now. He would only think she was raving.

Disgust registered on the weathered face. "You're one of the summer people?"

"Yes."

"And you were on one of them fancy boats?" It sounded like an indictment.

"I was," she admitted, trembling with shock and cold.

"Dude sailormen," the elderly man said angrily. "Hardly any of them know what they're doing. The waters around here are crowded with boats and nobody knows how to operate them!"

The other man returned with blankets and solicitously wrapped them around her. She felt their warmth and relaxed a little though she continued to tremble some.

The elderly man asked, "Whose boat was it?"

"Greg Carter's."

He scowled. "I know the Carters. The family used to live here. They still own Blue Gables and come here in the summertime. One of them was killed in an accident not long ago."

"Yes," she said.

"You know the name of the craft?" he asked.

She was lucky enough to remember. *The Norway Lady*, she said.

"I'll send a message right off," the elderly man said. "I'll alert the Coast Guard and send out a general message. We'll get word to them some way and let them know you're safe."

"Thanks," she said.

"We're on our way in to Dark Harbor," the elderly man told her. "You'd better go below and stay in one of the bunks until we get there."

She was ready to agree to anything and allowed the other man to help her down below. There in the warm quarters lit by a swaying lantern she stretched out on a good-sized bunk. The man saw that she was comfortable and covered with blankets before he left her.

She lay there slowly returning to full consciousness. She was vaguely aware of the motion of the boat which appeared to be a large but venerable fishing craft. The lantern swung lazily above her and she closed her eyes to try and concentrate and get it all straight in her mind.

There could be no doubt that she'd been the victim of a ghostly Elise. The others had all been in the forward area of the craft. And she had been standing there alone, a target for the phantom. She knew that Mort would be angry and scoff at her story and she couldn't imagine what Greg's attitude would be. She also doubted that Kay had seen anything, since the last time she'd observed her, the girl had been huddled in a chair in the cabin with her eyes closed. It turned out that Kay had a queasy stomach which could not endure the calmest of oceans.

The throb of the boat's engines pounded in her ears. Time passed and she still lay there awake. Then she heard someone come down into the cabin. She opened her eyes to see that it was the elderly man who was apparently in command of the fishing boat.

He stood by the bunk and told her, "The Coast Guard just answered us. They've been in touch with *The Norway Lady*. I guess that Greg Carter was almost out of his mind. Anyhow his worries are over now. He knows we found you and he'll be waiting to greet you when we dock."

"How long will that be?" she asked.

"An hour or a little more," he told her. "Better try and rest."

"I will," she promised.

He left her alone again and the heat and the throbbing engines finally allowed her to doze. Then when she was on the brink of a true sleep, the elderly man returned to announce that they were about to dock. The period after that remained one of confusion and misery for her.

She recalled the elderly man helping her up on the wharf and a gaunt-faced Greg coming forward to take her in his arms. He lifted her up and carried her to the station wagon where the others were waiting. He made her stretch out on the back seat while he and the other two sat in the front for the drive back to Blue Gables.

Kay gazed over the seat back to tell her, "I blamed myself for not being with you, but I was so ill."

"It wasn't your fault," she said dully as the station wagon sped along.

Mort asked her, "What happened?"

"Later," she said. "I don't want to think about it now."

At the wheel Greg said, "I've already phoned Dr. Taylor and he's waiting at the house for us."

"You shouldn't have," she protested.

"Don't be ridiculous," Greg said. "Being in the icy water that way after your accident could bring on any number of complications."

"I'll be all right after a warm bath," she said weakly.

And as it turned out that was the first thing Dr. Taylor prescribed for her. When she'd soaked in the hot water and was safely between the sheets in her own bed, he gave her a thorough examination.

When he finished, he said, "You seem to have come out of

this remarkably well. You don't even have a temperature."

Propped against pillows, she said, "I'm glad of that."

"It's a miracle you're alive," Dr. Taylor told her gravely.

"I know."

"Few people tumble into the ocean at night and are found. If that fishing boat hadn't come along you wouldn't have had any hope."

"I was ready to give up when I saw its lights," she agreed.

Dr. Henry Taylor closed his small black doctor's bag. "First you survive head injuries in that car accident and now you escape being drowned. I hope there won't be a third happening. You mightn't be so lucky next time."

"I'll remember that," she promised.

He gave her a searching look. "How did you come to fall into the water?"

She hesitated. Then she said, "I guess I sort of lost my balance. The boat lurched suddenly."

"You'd better be more careful in future."

"I will be."

He got up with a sigh. "I'll drop by tomorrow just to make sure no complications turn up."

"You needn't," she said. "I'm sure I'm going to be all right."

The old doctor chuckled. "I guess maybe you will be. You've seemingly been given a cat's nine lives. Nothing else that I know explains it."

He left her and Aunt Madge came in to fuss over her. The old woman said, "You poor dear, it's a miracle you weren't drowned. Greg and that precious boat! It's a silly toy with him."

It took several minutes to get rid of the fretful old lady and then Greg arrived to sit with her. His handsome face showed the grim torment he'd experienced.

Taking her hand in his, he said, "I'm so grateful you're alive I don't know what to say."

She managed a forlorn smile. "Don't worry about words. I understand."

There was pain in his eyes as he said, "When I think of you out there struggling alone in that dark, icy water it makes me ill."

"I survived."

"That's surely a miracle," he said. "Without that fishing boat coming along you'd have surely drowned."

"I know," she said. "When did you miss me?"

"Mort went back to see if you were all right. Kay was ill in the cabin and he began to worry that maybe you'd become sick as well. He came back and said he couldn't find you."

"What then?"

"I was in a panic. I secured the wheel and joined with Mort in searching for you. It took only a few minutes to learn you weren't on the boat. We went back to the cabin and told Kay."

"What did she say?"

"She became hysterical," Greg said grimly. "By that time I was cursing the day I ever set foot on that boat, let alone took you on it."

"I'm sorry," she said.

Greg studied her with tortured eyes and asked, "What really did happen? I didn't want to talk about it until I knew you were all right."

Quietly she said, "I guessed that."

"Tell me," he urged her.

"I was shoved overboard."

"What?" His eyes widened.

"That's what happened," she said in an even voice. "I was standing in the bow and suddenly a ghost appeared. The ghost of Elise!"

149

His expression was gaunt. "Go on!"

"I was naturally shocked. I tried to dodge back. Before I could manage it she attacked me and sent me toppling into the ocean."

There was a short silence. And in a strange voice he said, "The ghost of Elise!"

"You know I've seen her before!"

"So you claimed."

"And it's true," she said anxiously. "I don't expect others to believe me but I think you should."

He stared at her. "I should?"

"You know the background of all that has happened. The ghosts of Elise and Grant have appeared here. It's because they have something to tell us. Something about the scandal that hasn't come to light."

Disbelief showed on his handsome face. "Is that why the ghost of Elise attacked you?"

"No, I think she did that because she was jealous of me in life and remains so in death."

"You expect me to believe that?"

"You probably will refuse to," she said unhappily. "But that is only because you prefer to close your eyes to the truth."

In that strangely subdued voice he said, "I'm going to surprise you this time. I'm going to agree that you were the victim of Elise's ghost."

It was her turn to show shock. "What makes you so ready to agree with me?" she asked.

He looked at her very directly. "Because I saw the ghost myself. I saw her for just a second or two reflected in the glass of the window on my left. I thought it was an illusion or my imagination. But taken together with what you've told me I know better."

Chapter Nine

Nina stared at the handsome young man in utter amazement. His admission of seeing Elise's ghost was the last thing she'd expected of him. And it added to her own conviction that the ghost was a very real consideration and not a figure conjured up by their fears.

In an awed voice she asked him, "Did you tell Mort what you saw?"

"No. It was just after that he came to me with word that you had vanished. I forgot about the other thing. Finding you was all I cared about."

"Perhaps that is just as well," she said quietly. "No need to disturb him further. He has continually rejected the idea of the ghost."

"I can't any longer," Greg said in a troubled voice. "I don't understand it. I can only believe that it has something to do with the witchcraft Val Cramer is practicing."

"So we come back to that again?"

"Why not?"

"I don't know," she said, her pretty face shadowed. "It seems such a medieval point of view. Surely the concept of restless souls is enough to explain the ghostly appearances."

"I'm not sure about anything now," he said. "I'm only grateful that you are alive."

"How is Kay?" she asked.

"Badly shaken. She was seasick most of the time out there.

I'm afraid the evening cruise wasn't much of a success."

She smiled wryly. "At least we all survived it. I need to think more about the ghost and what her appearances mean. I'm sure they are linked with the scandal."

"You keep dredging up the scandal," he complained. "I wish you wouldn't. I can't see that this has anything to do with it."

"Let me have my own opinion, please," she said wearily. "I think you'd better go now. I'm very tired."

"Of course," he apologized at once. And he leaned over to kiss her tenderly. "Forgive me for not being more considerate. Tonight I learned that I truly love you."

She looked up at his adoring face and felt a sense of guilt. She wished that she could feel the same love for him but she didn't.

"I'm sorry you had such a bad time when you found me missing," she told him. "It's over with now. Try to forget about it."

"I'll never forget that half-hour before we received word from the Coast Guard that you had been rescued," Greg said grimly. "It's burned into my memory."

He left her and she put out the lights and tried to sleep. But sleep was delayed by the surge of tortured thoughts which swept through her mind. What had the ordeal of the night really signified? How long before she would encounter the ghost of Elise again? Once before she'd been close to drowning in the pool. It had been Bettina Wells who had rescued her then. She began wondering if perhaps she might do well to take Bettina up on her offer to hold a séance.

She had never taken any interest in séances before, but the older woman's offer to put her in touch with the spirits of Elise and Grant seemed too good an opportunity to miss. She decided that she would get in touch with Bettina and arrange a séance for a little later on.

With this thought uppermost in mind she dropped off to sleep. When she awoke in the morning she felt much better. It was a beautiful cool day with tangy, clear air and bright sun. It seemed impossible to her that she'd had the weird experiences of the night before. Yet she knew that she had.

Downstairs Aunt Madge Carter was especially solicitous of her. She said with an annoyed sniff, "One of the Cape television stations called and wanted to interview you. I told them you weren't feeling well enough."

"Thank you," Nina said.

The old woman frowned. "Word has spread about your close call. It's in all the morning papers and I suppose we'll be bothered by other curiosity seekers. It's not bad enough that you're almost drowned, they have to make a carnival out of it."

"Surely it won't be too bad," Nina protested. It was something she'd never thought about.

"The man who called from the radio and television station said they were interviewing some Captain Larsen on the air. I guess he's the one who rescued you."

"It's very likely. Let him have the publicity. He deserves some commendation for what he did."

"Just so long as they leave you alone," Aunt Madge Carter said sternly. "You let me take care of all the incoming calls. I'll protect you."

Nina also found the mood of the others solicitous. Greg was dictating to Kay when she passed the study and he stopped to come out and ask her if she felt all right. She assured him that she did and told him not to worry. After she'd had breakfast she went out on the stone patio.

It was out there that the big, moon-faced Mort Venn came

to join her. He was clad only in the red bathing trunks which made him look even larger than he was.

He paused to say, "I'm on my way to the pool."

"It's a good day for a swim," Nina agreed.

His round face looked bleak. "I guess you've had enough swimming for a while."

"I've had enough ocean swimming at least," she agreed wryly. "I might decide to join you in the pool later."

"I wouldn't expect it," the big man said uneasily. "Not after last night."

"I'm almost ready to forget it," she told him, though she wasn't being too truthful. She knew she would always remember the ordeal and the ghostly events leading up to it.

He gave her a grim look. "I'll never forget it," he promised. "A funny thing! Just before it happened I had a weird feeling."

Her attention was captured. "A weird feeling?"

"Yes," the big man said. "It was like a kind of fear came over me without any reason. I didn't know you were missing then, though perhaps it was that feeling that made me go look for you."

"I see."

"It was almost as if I'd been touched by a cold, phantom hand. I actually shivered."

She listened tensely, recalling her own experiences of that moment and of Greg telling her that he'd seen the reflection of Elise's pale ghost in the glass by the wheel. In a taut voice, she asked him, "Did you see anything?"

"No," he said. "This was just a feeling, a kind of impression. It's hard to explain. Perhaps it was some psychic warning that you were in danger."

"Perhaps," she said, feeling a familiar chill down her spine once again. "Speaking of the psychic. What is your opinion of Bettina as a medium?"

The stout man frowned. "Bettina Wells?"

"Yes."

"I have no idea," he said. "I know there is some sort of mumbo jumbo going on over there but I put Val Cramer and his effigies down as the offenders. I've only known Bettina as a rather good publicity woman not as a medium."

"She claims to have powers."

Mort looked skeptical. "A typical British woman of her class. A lot of them claim to have clairvoyant powers. They'll do anything from reading tea leaves, to studying your palm and gazing into a crystal ball. I don't put any stock in it."

"You're probably right," she said. "Don't let me keep you from the pool."

"We'll have a talk later," the stout man promised as he headed for the pool with a towel over his arm.

He had barely gone before Dr. Taylor drove up. Seeing her on the patio he came straight to her without entering the house.

Smiling at her, he said, "You look wonderful this morning. You discourage me. I never have you as a patient for long."

"That is because your treatments are so effective," she said.

He sat with her. "No ill effects from last night at all?"

"Just the scary memory of it. It will take time to lose that."

He nodded. "No question of that. I'm still puzzled as to just how you came to topple out of the boat. You never did explain that to my satisfaction. The ocean was calm last night."

She tried to seem casual as she replied, "I'm sure it was my own stupidity. I leaned over the side too far. I've had little boating experience."

The white-haired Dr. Taylor said dryly, "You added to it last night."

"I surely did," she agreed.

He stood up. "Well, no use wasting my time here when I'm on call elsewhere. You'll let me know if you need me, won't you?"

"I promise," she said, rising to see him on his way.

As soon as he drove off, she went into the house and looked up Bettina Wells' number. She reached the older woman who at once subjected her to a torrent of questions about the near-drowning.

"I'm perfectly all right," she told the woman at the other end of the line, "but I would like to see you after lunch if it's convenient."

"What about?" Bettina asked, in a voice which betrayed nervousness.

"I'd like to discuss a séance with you," she said. "There were things about last night which I don't understand. I think they might be explained in a séance."

"You gave me the impression you didn't believe in trying to reach the spirit world," Bettina Wells said.

"I have changed my mind," Nina said. "Can I come over around two o'clock?"

"If you like," Bettina said without much enthusiasm. "I'll be watching the studio for Val. You can join me there. When he returns we can go back to the cottage and have a talk."

Nina quickly accepted this arrangement, as she felt that if she didn't the older woman might not see her at all. Bettina was all at once showing a different attitude toward her. This puzzled her, and she wondered if it had anything to do with the previous night's happenings.

At lunch she told Mort that she was going to visit Bettina.

"I'm meeting her at the studio," she explained.

The big man looked worried. "If I were you I'd keep away from there. I'm afraid of those people."

She smiled at him in mild amazement. "I've never heard you say anything like that before."

He looked embarrassed. "I'm probably wildly wrong. But it's my feeling there's something not right over there."

Because she knew the Cramers and Bettina were controversial, she didn't mention her planned visit to Greg or his Aunt Madge. She was certain that they would have objections and she'd already made up her mind to go there.

Just a little before two she slipped out a side door of the great mansion and began the walk to the studio. She made her way inside and gave a tiny shudder as she passed the effigy of Marilyn Monroe in one of the alcoves and the sturdy figure of Captain Zachary Miller in the other. It seemed that Val Cramer had decided to decorate the alcoves with his figures once again.

When she entered the workshop she found Bettina there talking with two middle-aged lady tourists. The blonde woman explained Val's art to them and took them on a tour of the inner room. Nina waited and inspected the bench of the artist. The single carving he was working on was a thin hand. She picked up the partially completed hand and noticed the thick veins outlined in it and the claw-like fingers. It was evidently the hand of someone very old. Just holding it gave her a strange sensation.

She put it down and glanced about the workroom. At the other side of the room and stretched out on a table was an effigy. She walked over to it with the voices of Bettina and the tourists coming to her from the other room. As she reached the table she was shocked to see that the effigy stretched out there was hers!

Val Cramer had completed the figure and there could be no question that it was lifelike. Her head had been adorned with a wig which exactly matched her own hair and he had placed a dark crimson robe on the effigy. A robe with full flowing lines. As she stared at the figure with a sense of horror she suddenly realized that the robe was wet!

There could be no doubt about it! She reached over and touched the robe with her fingers and it was sopping wet! Her eyes wandered in horror to the lifelike face of the effigy and she wondered at the coincidence. Last night she'd almost drowned and today she had come upon this soaked likeness of herself.

A footstep sounded behind her and she turned in alarm to look up into the Lincolnesque mask of Val Cramer. The artist's weathered face with its bearded chin showed a cold smile.

"This is the first time you've seen the completed figure," he said.

"Yes," she managed in a small voice as her eyes returned to the figure. "I don't understand why the robe is so wet."

"I just took it out of a dye rinse," he said. "The color of the robe wasn't right. I wanted it an exact shade to match the skin tones and the hair color. The easiest way was to dip the gown in the dye while it was draped on the figure."

"I see," she said, not at all convinced by his explanation. It seemed to her it must have to do with something else—like her being shoved into the ocean by the blonde phantom. Had Val Cramer managed the macabre drama by manipulating the effigies here in his studio?

The tourists and Bettina came back into the workroom. Both women bought small carvings from the artist. He was still wrapping them up when Bettina and Nina left the studio. Not until they reached the shadowed living room of the cottage did they begin to talk.

Nina began with, "I saw my effigy in the workshop. I was shocked to find it drenched."

Bettina's strong features showed uneasiness. She said, "He spoke of changing the color of the robe. Perhaps he put it in the dye solution this morning."

"That is what he told me," she said.

The blonde woman made a tiny gesture of dismissal. "Then that explains it."

"I wonder," she said.

Bettina's sharp blue eyes fixed on her. "Wonder what?"

"It doesn't really matter," she replied. "I've come here today to ask if you'll hold a séance for me."

"Right away?"

"Why not?"

"I need preparation," Bettina Wells said. "Whom do you want to try and reach?"

"Grant Carter and Elise Venn."

"You're still trying to delve into that scandal?"

"Yes," she said firmly.

The blonde woman stood facing her, her hands at her sides, nervously opening and closing them as if in uneasy deliberation. At last the older woman said, "I don't think you should try to invoke their spirits."

"Why not?"

"It could make you unhappy."

"What do you mean?"

Bettina hesitated, then she said, "I mean it's likely they were lovers. Better that you should remain in doubt than be faced with a cruel truth."

"I don't see it that way."

"No?"

"No. I'm interested in finding out the whole truth. Not

only whether they were lovers but who was responsible for the scandal surrounding them."

"Haven't you enough problems without that?" Bettina asked.

"Regardless of my problems, I came here on a mission and I'm not giving up at this point."

Bettina's face looked pale even in the dim light of the shuttered living room. She said, "You may be placing yourself in danger with this attitude."

"Then let me risk the danger," she told the older woman. "Will you sit with your crystal ball now and try to reach either of those two."

The blonde woman showed fear. "I'm almost certain to fail. I need to work myself up to it."

"You can try," she said firmly.

Bettina sighed and moved over to the table and lifted a black cloth to reveal a large glass sphere. She stared at her from above the crystal and warned, "Reaching the other side is not as easy as it may seem."

"I'm prepared for that," Nina told her.

"You're not a true believer," Bettina complained as she bent over the crystal and turned on a light below it which sent up a bright glow, giving it a strange, unearthly quality.

"Very impressive," Nina said.

"Sit opposite me facing the crystal," the older woman told her.

She did, then asked, "Now what?"

"I want you to concentrate," Bettina said. "Think of Grant Carter. Empty your mind of everything else."

"That will not be hard," she said in a taut voice, feeling a new, strange mood coming over her. It was extremely easy to be impressed by the shadowed room, the bright crystal and the pale face of Bettina as she cupped her hands over the glass ball and stared into its depths.

"I must have time," Bettina said in an eerie voice. "I think you are wrong to probe into these matters. It can only bring you misfortune."

"I've had more than my share of that already," Nina said with bitterness.

"Look deep into the crystal and think of Grant," Bettina commanded her.

"Mother!" the word spoken in a tone of loud disapproval shot across the room. In the next moment the dark room was flooded with electric light.

Startled, Nina turned to see an irate Jeri Cramer standing just inside the door by the light switch. Bettina said, "You've interrupted our séance."

The pert Jeri in summer shorts and blouse came over to them with fire in her hazel eyes. "That's exactly what I meant to do!"

Bettina was gazing up at her daughter in confusion. "I didn't expect you back so early."

"That's obvious," the pretty dark-haired girl said giving her mother an angry glance.

"Nina asked me to conduct the séance," the blonde woman explained.

"And I want no more of that going on here," Jeri snapped at her. "You know Val objects to your séances!"

"He needn't know," her mother said.

"He'll know because I'll tell him," the dark girl continued. She turned to Nina and added, "I should think you'd have better sense than to get mixed up in anything like this."

Nina got up from her chair. "I hoped it might turn out to be an interesting experiment," she said awkwardly.

Jeri's pert face was full of scorn. "You were trying to take advantage of my mother."

161

"Not really," she protested.

"I know better," the dark girl said. "You can go someplace else if you want to indulge in séances. There won't be any held here."

"I'm sorry," Nina said. "I didn't realize you had such strong feelings about it."

"Well, you know now! Under the circumstances I think you'd better go."

Nina was startled by Jeri's anger and also by the strangely subservient manner of the girl's mother. Bettina stood by the crystal ball looking thoroughly chastened with her head down.

Nina said, "I surely didn't want to start any family quarrels. I'm sorry it turned out this way."

"I wonder," Jeri said with obvious sarcasm.

Nina made her way out of the cottage and headed for Blue Gables. She was still stunned by Jeri's behavior. The reason she had given had been that she and Val were totally opposed to séances. But Nina knew this was not so. There had to be more to it.

Greg was standing by the stables when she returned. He waved and motioned for her to join him. She did and he studied her.

"You were over to the studio?"

"Yes."

"You've had phone calls," he said, looking more like Grant than usual as he stood there in the bright sunshine. "You ought to let us know when you're going out."

"I didn't expect to be gone long. Were the calls important?"

A small smile crossed his handsome, tanned face. "They were from the press. Mother took care of them."

"She said she would."

"It seems she's very good at it," Greg said. He glanced over at the studio in the distance. "What went on over there?"

"Nothing much."

His eyebrows arched. "Aren't you being very mysterious today?"

"I don't intend to be."

"Who did you see?"

"All of them."

"And you have nothing to tell me?" He sounded disbelieving.

She'd made up her mind not to mention the wet robe on her effigy to him. She'd decided to wait and discuss it later. So she said, "No. There were some tourists there and it was all very casual."

"I see." Again he sounded doubtful. "I'll be going to the mainland for a few days. I'm leaving in the morning. Would you like to go out somewhere for dinner tonight? We could pick a fairly private spot."

She felt embarrassed. "Sorry. I've already promised to go to dinner with Derek Mills."

Greg stared at her. "After all that happened last night? You oughtn't to leave here."

"You just invited me out," she reminded him.

"That was different," he said unhappily.

"I fail to see the difference."

"When did you tell Derek you'd meet him?"

"Before last night."

"Then he wouldn't expect you to keep the date," Grant said. "He'd realize it isn't sensible."

"He hasn't called yet so I'll expect him. I have an idea he's met Dr. Taylor somewhere and found out that I'm no worse for my adventure."

Greg showed chagrin. "You're stubborn," was his comment.

"I suppose so," she said cheerfully. "I don't think it is always a bad quality."

"Do what you please!" Greg said with a return of the old sullenness which had originally made her distrust him. And he walked away.

Nina found that Greg was not the only one to disapprove of her going out. Aunt Madge Carter sputtered and fumed about it. Mort Venn expressed his wonder at her wanting to appear in public so soon and Kay seemed awed by her remarkable stamina.

Kay knocked on the door of Nina's room while she was dressing. Comb in hand she went to the door and opened it. Seeing Kay she invited her in.

"They're all raving downstairs," the girl announced with a shy smile.

"About my having a date tonight?"

"Yes."

"I feel all right. There's no reason for me to break it."

Kay said, "I guess not. They don't seem to understand. I'd never be able to go out tonight if I'd gone through what you did."

She turned to the dark girl with a smile as she finished with her hair. "You didn't exactly have a good time. You were so ill and then you must have had some strain when you were told I was missing."

"I thought I would die," Kay confessed. "To hear that and be so ill at the same time."

"Don't think about it," she said. "I'm not."

"Your dress looks lovely," Kay said.

"Thanks." She had worn a rose gown with bright metallic trim at the waist. It was one of her favorites and she wore it whenever her spirits needed a lift.

Kay stood by the door. "I won't keep you. I hear you were over at the studio today."

"Yes," she said. "I found everyone there in rather a strange mood."

"Oh?" the dark-haired Kay showed interest.

"I'll tell you more about it later," she told the girl. "I felt that Bettina was almost frightened."

"That's strange."

"I thought so. Jeri seems to have great authority over her. There are times when I think those two may have been the ones to help Senator Ryan build that scandal against Grant and Elise."

Kay's face showed alarm. "But Mr. Venn doesn't think so, and he employed the mother."

"Mort Venn isn't the brightest man alive," Nina told the other girl.

"I know," Kay agreed.

"He might easily have been fooled by those two," she said. Before she could continue, Aunt Madge came up to say that Derek Mills had arrived. The old woman studied her rather grimly and said, "Well, you've made yourself attractive enough for him."

"Thank you," she said with a small laugh and hurried on her way.

Derek Mills was waiting on the patio in a white suit. He smiled as she appeared and said, "If I hadn't met Dr. Taylor I would have been sending you flowers and my condolences."

"I thought you must have seen him," she said.

Derek led her to his car. "The doctor told me there was no reason at all you couldn't dine with me tonight. So here I am."

After they were in the car and driving out the shore road he announced, "You made headlines in all the papers this morning."

"I know," she said.

"Did the reporters give you a bad time?"

"It would have been worse if Miss Carter hadn't taken it on herself to protect me."

Derek's face showed amusement as he kept his eyes on the road. "She's just the one to do it. You're like a creature recovered from the sea. You'll be a legend around here."

"It was a hard way to gain fame," she said.

"I want to hear all about it," he told her.

"You will," she promised him. She had decided he would be her confidant. She'd not really told anyone everything yet. The young museum director was the person whom she trusted most and so it seemed he was the logical one to know the details.

They drove along the shore road and he pointed out his house, a large Victorian building, in well-kept condition. After they passed it he seemed in a more somber mood.

Glancing at him, she said, "You seem worried."

"I had rather bad news today," he said. After a short pause he went on, "You must have heard my wife is in a mental hospital on the mainland."

"Yes, I have," she said quietly.

Keeping his eyes on the road he went on, "Yesterday she tried to take her life and almost succeeded. I received word last night. I was going over to see her but the doctor advised me against it. For some reason my presence always seems to upset her more."

"I'm so sorry," she said.

"Thank you," he said in a small voice. "I've been alone in that big house so long that merely the sight of it makes me upset."

She looked at his tense young face and felt great sympathy for him. She said, "Is there any chance of her recovering?"

"It seems there is very little. But one keeps hoping."

"I know," she said.

"Some new treatment may turn up. The doctors tell me that. But meanwhile her physical condition has gone down. I've almost resigned myself to losing her."

"Probably that is wise," she said.

They came to the sprawling restaurant which was situated close to the water with many of the tables facing the ocean. The hostess at once recognized Derek and showed them to an excellent table with a good view of the sea.

Derek smiled across the table at Nina. "I imagine we can both do with a drink," he said.

"I can," she told him.

He ordered and then said, "Tell me about last night."

"It's a long story," she warned him.

"I want to hear it all."

She began and before she was half-way through the waitress brought their drinks. When she came to the part where the ghost of Elise appeared and shoved her over the side, she warned him, "This you'll find hard to accept."

"Go on."

She took a sip of her drink, then said, "I was standing in the stern alone when suddenly out of the shadows a ghost with flowing blonde hair appeared. I knew at once it was Elise. Before I could do anything but scream, she came at me and pushed me over into the water."

Derek stared at her over his drink and gave a small gasp. "The blonde phantom again?"

"Yes."

"You're certain?"

"There's no doubt in my mind."

Derek frowned and said, "Did you tell this to anyone else?"

"Only to one other person."

"Who?"

"Greg."

"What was his reaction?"

She sat back with a grimace. "Not at all what I expected," she confessed. "I thought he would make light of it or at least dispute it."

"And?"

"He didn't," she said, looking at Derek, her eyes troubled. "He admitted that later, apparently after I went overboard, he saw the reflection of Elise's ghost in one of the windows on the bridge."

"What about Mort and Kay?"

"Kay was in the cabin seasick. She was helpless."

"And Mort?"

"He didn't see anything and Greg didn't tell him about his experience nor did I. But without hearing our stories he told me that he'd had a strange feeling just before he went looking for me. He'd suddenly found himself afraid. As if a ghost had brushed by him."

Derek gasped. "Then all three of you shared some supernatural experience?"

She gave the museum director an earnest look. "That is the way it seems. Of course Greg is still suspicious of Val Cramer and the spells he may be working. Because of that I went over there today."

"Did you learn anything?" Derek asked.

"I don't know," she said grimly. "I can only tell you that the effigy he'd made of me was resting on a table and the gown that was on it was water-soaked!"

Chapter Ten

"Interesting," Derek Mills said.

Nina sighed. "He had a perfectly logical explanation for it. According to him the gown on the effigy had not been the right shade and he'd just dipped it in a dye solution."

"Perhaps he was telling the truth," Derek said.

"I know. I'm inclined to give him the benefit of the doubt. Yet one wonders."

The museum director's intelligent face was serious. He told her, "I've been doing a lot of thinking about it all. Val Cramer is a strange person. And it has occurred to me he might have caused some of these ghost appearances by using the effigies he has constructed."

She listened with a slight frown. "Meaning what?"

"It would seem within the realm of possibility that he could move about in the darkness with one of those figures held before him. No one takes a second look at a ghost. Just the sight of a woman's figure with flowing blonde hair would be enough to suggest that it was a phantom Elise."

"I've never thought of that," she agreed. "I've been mostly concerned that he had some black magic method of manipulating the effigies to cause things to happen to their real counterparts."

"It could be much more simple and direct than that," he argued. "If Cramer merely moved those effigies around in the night so they'd be seen at various times and places the ghostly legends could be started."

"What about on the boat?"

"He might have been concealed somewhere below and used the effigy to mask his attack on you when he appeared at the stern. Later, in the excitement over your disappearance, he could escape to the wharf after the boat docked."

"I hadn't thought of that," she admitted. "But Greg claims he and Mort made a thorough search of the craft when they were looking for me. Wouldn't they have come upon Val Cramer if he were hidden there with the effigy?"

"Not necessarily," Derek said. "The craft is large enough so that he might move from one place of concealment to another. He could be overlooked."

"It's an interesting theory," she said. "I'd like to discuss it with Greg."

"Not likely he'll agree with it," the museum director predicted.

"You can't tell," she said.

The waitress came and took their orders. Nina glanced out the window and saw that fog was settling over the ocean and drifting in toward the island.

She said, "It appears the fog is going to be thick again."

"It's been predicted," he said, also glancing out the window. "If it lingers through tomorrow I'd advise you against driving."

"You don't need to warn me," she assured him with a wry smile. "I've learned my lesson."

"And last night must have been a terrifying experience," he said.

"It was. I was close to drowning."

"I didn't know about it until this morning," Derek said. "By that time you'd been rescued and it was all history. Then I met Dr. Taylor and he told me you'd not really suffered from it at all."

"That's not quite the truth," she said. "I have a scar on my mind which will always be there."

The brown-haired young man gave her a searching look. "Do you plan to remain here after all this?"

"I feel I can't leave yet."

"Because of your wish to clear Grant's name?"

"Yes."

"Are you getting anywhere with it?"

"It doesn't seem so," she said. "And yet I have the feeling that something will break to reveal the truth fairly soon. I intend to talk to Bettina Wells. I have reason to believe she knows more about what happened than she's been willing to admit. Further, I'm sure her daughter, Jeri, is aware of this and keeping a stern watch on her mother to see that she keeps silent."

Derek Mills looked mildly surprised. "You think the daughter knows something?"

"I'm certain of it," she said and told him how Jeri had stopped her mother from conducting a séance.

The young man listened with obvious interest. "That does suggest something," he agreed.

"The strange thing is that Bettina actually seemed afraid of her daughter."

"That could be for another reason," Derek pointed out. "She may know something of her son-in-law's black magic activities and feel she has grounds to fear those young people."

"Greg thinks they are up to some mischief and he's almost won over Mort Venn to his way of thinking."

"I'm rather surprised that Mort Venn is remaining so long at the Carters as a guest," Derek said.

"So am I. Perhaps it's because he's never really recovered from his wife's suicide."

"It was a tragic affair," Derek agreed.

"I don't think it was a suicide," she went on. "That is part of what I've discovered. She'd been drinking at the time and I believe she fell from that balcony rather than jumped from it."

"Have you discussed it with him?"

"Yes."

"What did he say?"

"He's not sure. I think I partly convinced him. It's important since it has a bearing on whether she and Grant were lovers or not. And I have never accepted that."

He studied her with sad amusement. "You don't give up easily, I'll say that for you. What next?"

"I'm going to see Bettina again and question her more. I'm also going to have her conduct a séance if I can. It may be ridiculous but I think some information could come from that."

"At this point you can try anything," he said. "But in view of these phantom attacks on you I worry about your remaining here."

"I'll have to take the chance."

"If you hadn't been found quickly last night it would have been all over," he reminded her.

"I know."

"You may face a similar danger again."

She grimaced. "That's a calculated risk. I'll simply have to live with it."

"Just so long as you live," the museum director said with grim meaning as their meal was brought in.

For a while they dropped the macabre subject and gave their attention to the excellent seafood dinner. She noticed that the fog was continuing to move in and that it was now almost dark outside.

As they sat over coffee at the end of their meal, she said, "I had no idea Pirate Island had so much fog."

"We've had more than usual this year and it has been more

dense," Derek said. "But the old timers tell stories of the days when sailing ships were locked in the mists just beyond the shoals for days on end. They dared not move in until the fog lifted."

"It must surely have been a problem," she agreed.

"Complicated by the fact that there is only a narrow entrance to the harbor," he said. "The harbor area itself is large but the passage from the ocean is small and full of hazardous shoals. We have had a few wrecks even in late years. Ships have been caught in clear weather and it's far more dangerous when it's foggy."

"I haven't seen Captain Miller lately," she said. "His effigy is still hanging over at Val Cramer's studio."

"Zachary isn't too delighted about that," Derek said, "but there isn't much he can do to stop it."

"I know," she agreed. "I feel in the same position. I'm supposed to be honored by my effigy, but I'm not sure that's true."

"Cramer is a strange person," Derek said. "I don't know what started him doing those effigies. Now they seem to be his main activity."

They left the restaurant and drove slowly through the fog back to Dark Harbor. There they stopped at a coffee house filled mostly with college age young men and women. A rock group sang requests and played noisily. Every once in a while they came up with an ancient sea chanty rendered in their strange new style.

They had a table far from the stage but even at that distance the music was much too loud. Nina gave Derek a meaningful look and said, "This may not be the best group that has ever played on the island, but it's surely the loudest."

Derek laughed. "Have you had enough?"

"I think so."

He glanced around the crowded, smoke-filled room with

its psychedelic lighting and said, "I wonder what the original islanders would say if they came back and heard this."

"They wouldn't believe it."

As he signalled to their waiter to bring the check, he turned to her. "It's getting late and you shouldn't stay out too long after your ordeal last night."

"I am beginning to feel weary," she admitted. And she saw by her wristwatch that it was close to eleven o'clock.

Outside the fog was steadily growing worse. The hilly main street of the town was cloaked in the mist so that you could hardly see the signs on the various storefronts. Even the neon lights were blurred. She noticed that they were almost directly across the street from the Gray Heron tavern and hotel.

Standing in the doorway of the hotel was Greg. He had come out as they were standing there and then had suddenly turned and gone back inside, as if he didn't want to meet them.

She turned to Derek in surprise and said, "Wasn't that Greg who just came out of the Gray Heron?"

The young man nodded. "I thought it was. He didn't stay there long enough for me to get a good look at him before he went inside."

"I'm certain it was him!" she insisted. "But I've never known him to visit the Gray Heron."

"I have never thought of him as a friend of Matt Kimble's," the young man agreed.

"He went back in there!"

"If it really was Greg."

"It was," she said. "Let's go over and find out what he's doing there and why he behaved so strangely."

Derek gave her a dubious look. "Do you think we should? We could be wrong."

"I don't think we are. And what is there to stop us going in to the place? It's a public saloon isn't it?"

"Yes. But they get only a certain class of clientele. We wouldn't ordinarily go in there."

"So what is Greg doing there?"

"I can't imagine," the young man said grimly.

"Let's try and find out," she told him.

She led the way across the cobblestoned street, wet and shining with moisture now, to the entrance of the tavern. It was poorly lighted for a public place and the glass of the door had been painted green so no one could see in. Derek opened the door and they stepped inside to a square room with a bar at the far end and a few circular tables with plain chairs around them.

Their entrance caused some interest. A group of unshaven fishermen in heavy workclothes was playing cards at the near table and they all turned to stare. There were no women in the tavern, Nina discovered as they walked to the bar where a few men were standing. The bartender was the dour Matt Kimble, and a look of annoyance crossed his big slab-face as they approached.

She said, "I'd like to speak with Greg Carter."

Matt Kimble glared at her. "He ain't here."

"But he must be!" she protested, glancing around without seeing any sign of Greg.

Derek spoke up, "Just a moment ago he stepped out in the doorway and then came back in here."

The big man behind the bar showed a look of disgust. He said, "You're wrong. No one left here or came back a moment ago. No one has stepped out of that door for the last quarter-hour."

They exchanged glances of disbelief. Then Derek told Matt Kimble. "We just saw him!"

"You made a mistake," Matt said, turning to serve a

customer a distance down the bar from them.

When he left them she turned to Derek in dismay and said, "He's lying to us."

"Maybe," the young man said indecisively. "The fog is thick. We could have been mistaken."

"We saw someone in the doorway. I'm sure it was Greg. And he says that no one went out. So he has to be lying."

"Likely," Derek said in an uneasy tone. "This is not a friendly place. I suggest we get on our way." And he took her by the arm and led her out of the murky drinking place.

When they reached the cool dampness of the fog-ridden night she turned unhappily to him. "Why do you think he lied to us?"

"I don't know," Derek admitted.

"The tavern is very run-down."

"I told you. It's a workingman's place. And the story is that Matt conducts some shady deals there. He is said to buy stolen goods and ship them to the mainland for sale."

"Sounds in character," she said unhappily as they stood on the sidewalk in the heavy fog.

Derek shrugged. "If he says Greg wasn't there, I guess he wasn't."

"In that case I saw someone who looked exactly like him," she said slowly. Her eyes challenged the young man. "Could I have seen Grant?"

"Grant is dead!"

"Exactly what I mean," she said. "Perhaps I saw a ghost."

"If you saw one so did I," the young man said unhappily. "I won't admit that we did. Let's get away from here."

They walked through the fog to the parking lot and got in Derek's car. It had been an eerie experience and she didn't know exactly what to make of it. In the end she decided not to persist as it seemed to frustrate Derek.

As Derek drove her to Blue Gables, he said, "We must see each other soon again."

"I hope we can," she agreed.

"If there's anything you think I can do to help, don't hesitate to call on me," he said, as they drove along in the dark, foggy night.

"I'll remember," she promised.

"I've enjoyed this evening," he said. "And I don't want anything to happen to you."

"I appreciate your interest," she said. "I've enjoyed having you as a friend."

They reached the front entrance of Blue Gables and he saw her to the door. He kissed her goodnight and saw her safely inside. She stood in the hallway for a moment as he drove away in the fog. As the red taillights of the car vanished she again wondered whether she'd seen Greg or not. And she decided to stop by his door and see if he was in his room.

There seemed to be no sign of anyone downstairs in the old mansion. The living room was in darkness, and she noticed through the French windows that the lights at the swimming pool were still on. This aroused her curiosity as to who might be out there in the dense fog. Of course the pool was kept heated and Greg or Mort could very well have decided to go out for a midnight swim.

She went to the French doors, opened them and stepped out on the patio. The pool lights had all been switched on but the pool seemed to be deserted. Puzzled by this, she moved across the wet grass to the pool and gazed into it. The moment she did, she froze with terror!

There floating beneath the surface of the pool was the phantom blonde! Elise had returned to haunt her from the pool. But even as she stared at the slim figure in the dark bathing suit, she began to have frantic second thoughts. It

177

was difficult to be certain, but this figure under the water didn't seem like the phantom who had appeared before, despite the streaming yellow hair.

She quickly turned and ran back into the house only to meet Greg, in his smoking jacket, coming down the hall from the study. The handsome man halted and stared at her. "What is wrong?" he demanded.

Her teeth were chattering with fright now and she had a difficult time stammering, "The pool—someone in it! Looks like Elise!"

His eyes widened. "Elise?" he exclaimed.

Before she could reply he brushed by her roughly and hurried to the still open French doors and out to the poolside. She raced after him. She saw him pause by the pool, then hurl off his smoking jacket and dive into the pool in his undershirt and trousers. She arrived in time to see him come splashing up from below the pool's surface with a body in his arms.

She stood there stiff with horror as he lifted the dripping body of the blonde woman out on the grass and then clambered out himself. He turned the body over and Nina found herself gazing into the horror-stricken face of Bettina Wells! The blonde woman's eyes were open and staring eerily, and the full red lips were wide as if in protest.

Greg got up from the body and gave her a dazed look. "It's Bettina!" he said. "She's done for!"

"No!"

He nodded grimly. "She must have come over here on her own to have a swim and taken some sort of seizure and drowned!"

"I can't believe it!"

Greg ran a hand through his matted, wet hair as he stood indecisively between her and the body. "I don't know what to do first. Call Dr. Taylor, I guess. She's dead, but the sooner he sees her the sooner he'll be able to decide what happened to her."

In a small voice, she said, "And the Cramers. They'll have to know."

"Yes," Greg agreed. "I'll get on the phone at once." He took her by the arm. "You can't stay out here alone with that."

"Should we leave her?"

He said bleakly, "No one can hurt her now!"

"No," she said, still dazed. "Your smoking jacket." It was still on the ground where he'd left it.

Greg gave her an odd look, but walked back dripping to pick up the jacket and place it over his arm. Then he returned and said, "While I'm on the phone you can wake Mort and Kay and let them know what has happened."

"What about your aunt?"

"If Aunt Madge manages to sleep through this, let her," was his decision. "Rouse the others!"

They hurried into the house and Greg headed for the phone while she rushed upstairs. It took several minutes rapping at Mort's door to waken the big man, but Kay proved to be a light sleeper and answered almost at once. Nina briefly told them what had happened and then went downstairs again.

She found Greg talking to the housekeeper, and this elderly woman in her kimono appeared to have grasped the situation with the alertness of a true islander. The housekeeper said, "I'd best go up to Miss Carter."

"That would be a good idea," Greg agreed. As the old woman hastened to the stairway he turned to Nina and said, "Did you wake the others?"

"Yes," she said, "They'll be down in a minute."

"I've sent the gardener out to put a covering over the body until the doctor comes," he said. "I'm going up to change into dry clothes. Don't you go out there!"

She nodded agreement and remained standing in the living

room as he vanished upstairs. She was still stunned and feeling miserable. The last thing she'd expected was this drowning of Bettina Wells! She had been counting on her help to clear up the mystery about Grant. Now this link had been lost. And she could expect no help from Jeri or Val Cramer.

Indeed the blonde woman's daughter had intruded and halted their séance, a séance which Nina felt would have been helpful in finding out the truth about Grant and Elise. She could not predict what the dark girl's attitude would be now that her mother was dead, but she didn't expect any cooperation from her.

Mort came down the stairs in his dressing gown followed by a shattered Kay. The two joined Nina in the living room and plied her with questions.

"I only know she was in the pool when I came home," she said, unhappily. The strain was telling on her. "She was at the bottom of the pool and I at once thought it was Elise's ghost."

Mort showed annoyance and glared at her from behind his horn-rimmed glasses. "That was a fool thing to think!"

Kay protested, "Let her tell her story, please!"

"That's all," she said. "Greg came and recovered the body from the pool. The doctor is on the way now. And the gardener is out guarding her body."

Mort gave a deep sigh. "What else can happen here? I thought last night would be the end of these mad experiences. But they seem to go on."

"This has been an accident," Kay reproved him. "Poor Bettina!"

"It was a stupid thing for her to do," Mort Venn said almost savagely. "Coming over here in the middle of the night to swim alone."

Nina said, "She enjoyed swimming at night. I remember her coming over here once before." And then the impact of it hit her. It had been Bettina who had arrived in time to rescue her the night someone had tried to drag her below the surface of the pool and drown her. Had Bettina received the same treatment, only with no one to arrive in time to help her?

Mort must have noticed the shock that had accompanied her thoughts. He looked at her oddly. "Now what's wrong with you?"

"Nothing," she said weakly. "I was just thinking of something."

He looked disgusted. "I suppose you'll be blaming this on ghosts!"

Kay brushed back stray locks of black hair and told him, "I think you're behaving rather badly. Someone is dead out there, someone who once worked for you."

Mort became silent and sank into one of the nearby easy chairs in a resigned manner. At the same time Greg came back down dressed in dry trousers and a shirt open at the neck.

He said, "Aunt Madge is awake and in a state. She blames me for not having had a fence installed around the pool and kept locked at night."

Kay said, "That would have been wise."

"Only trespassers could get near the pool," Greg replied. "It didn't seem necessary."

Then the doctor came and shortly after Jeri and Val Cramer. Jeri seemed to be in a state of shock, but she bore up well, and Val went around asking tedious questions of everyone. Nina felt he made a needless nuisance of himself. Later Dr. Taylor came back inside and stated that death had been from drowning. He offered the opinion that the blonde woman must have had some sort of weak spell.

"Very foolish for anyone to swim alone," he said in summing up. "It's too bad this tragic thing had to happen."

Jeri collapsed in tears, and Val saw her to a nearby chair

and talked to her in an effort to calm her. The doctor crossed the room to where Nina was standing.

The white-haired man said, "After the miraculous escape you had from drowning I think it ironic that someone should be drowned here within a few yards of the house."

"I know," she said. She wanted to mention her narrow escape in the pool but felt it was neither the time nor the place.

He was studying her closely. "You look very pale. Do you feel well?"

"I'm all right," she said. "Just shaken by what has happened. Bettina was my friend."

"An interesting woman," the doctor agreed. "Well, it's too bad. I'd better chat with the daughter and make sure she has something to make her sleep."

Dr. Taylor went over to talk to Jeri and Val, and Nina found herself standing alone at the fireplace. After a moment Greg came down to her and said, "You look ill. You'd better get to bed."

"In a little while," she said.

Greg gazed grimly at the others clustered at the opposite end of the room. He said, "Jeri and Val seem badly shocked by this."

"No wonder."

He said, "Did you mention anything about what happened before?"

Her eyes met his. "You mean the night that Bettina rescued me in the pool?"

"Yes."

"No. I've said nothing about it."

"Best not to."

"I almost drowned. Something or someone pulled me under the water."

Greg looked sarcastic. "I remember. That was the night you were seeing ghosts."

"Don't make light of it!" she protested.

"Sorry," he said, with a scowl. "I just think now would be a poor time to talk about that night. This was a simple accident and we don't want to make it seem more."

She again searched his tired face. "Are you sure?"

"Of course. Do you have any doubts?"

"I haven't made up my mind yet."

"Just don't say anything like that to the others," he begged her. "Especially not to Aunt Madge."

Nina said, "There could be people who wanted Bettina dead. People who feared she might talk too much about Grant's campaign and bare some truths which have been concealed."

"I don't believe that," he said.

"I don't ask you to," she replied. "I'm only saying what's in my own mind."

"As long as you keep those thoughts to yourself," he advised her harshly.

Now she suddenly remembered the incident at the Gray Heron Tavern and she asked him, "Were you in Dark Harbor tonight?"

"No. I didn't leave the house. Why do you ask?" Greg answered, giving her an uneasy glance.

"I was certain I saw you."

"Where?"

"Coming out of the Gray Heron."

"That run-down tavern?" he exclaimed. "I never go near the place."

"I was sure it was you," she said.

He scowled again. "Grant used to go there occasionally. He had a friendship with Matt Kimble. I don't think I've been in the tavern more than twice in my life. And then I was with Grant."

"I see," she said. "Then I must have been mistaken."

"Badly mistaken," he said. "I'm going to suggest that everyone go to their rooms and get some rest. Val and Jeri can stay here the night if they wish."

As it turned out, Bettina's daughter and son-in-law preferred to return home. The others went up to bed while the gardener remained with the body waiting for the undertaker. Nina found it difficult to sleep. She lay in the darkness of her room staring up at the ceiling, tormented by fears and doubts.

She felt that Bettina's drowning had not been an accident as Dr. Taylor had declared, but she knew there was small chance of proving this. Somehow she felt the death of the blonde woman was linked to her own quest on the island for the true facts concerning Grant and Elise. She would continue to believe this until she was presented with facts which proved otherwise.

And all at once she was suspicious of Greg. She was almost certain she'd seen him in Dark Harbor and that he had some reason for concealing this. He'd also revealed himself as rather cruel in his attitude toward Bettina's drowning—almost as if he were glad that it had happened.

There was one macabre alternative to her having seen Greg at the entrance of the tavern. She might have seen Grant's ghost! Perhaps on this foggy night when death had again struck someone down at Blue Gables, the phantom figure of her beloved Grant had risen from his watery grave to stalk his favorite haunts in the old island village. Captain Zachary Miller had declared that this could happen and she was beginning to believe the old man's words. She made up her mind to see the venerable mariner again at her earliest opportunity.

Finally she fell asleep and in a tormenting nightmare dreamed the horror of discovering Bettina's body all over again. Only this time the corpse of the blonde woman came alive, pointed an accusing finger at Greg, and called him her murderer! Nina woke to a foggy morning feeling weary and ill.

Aunt Madge Carter was at the breakfast table when Nina went into the dining room. The old woman at once launched into a long dissertation on the drowning, again blaming Greg for not having fenced the pool.

"I shall have a fence around it before the week is out," she declared, her pale face showing annoyance. "I called Mr. Jenkins, the carpenter this morning."

"It would be a good safety measure," she agreed.

"A little late for that woman," Aunt Madge complained. "I didn't like her but I don't care to feel I was partly responsible for her death."

"I don't think you should blame anyone," she said. "It was her own decision to come here at night alone to swim."

"The funeral is going to be held here on the island," Aunt Madge said. "I'm a trifle surprised. I thought they would likely take the body back to Boston."

"Do they have a family plot here?"

"No. And that means they'll have to arrange with the church to get one," the old woman said with a frown. "The old burying ground is pretty well filled. Not too many summer people are buried here these days."

"Perhaps they think it is the simplest way," Nina said. "This is a very hard time for them."

The old woman looked grim as she took a sip of her coffee. "I wouldn't put it past that artist that he worked some spell on her. I haven't a doubt that he had her effigy over there in his collection."

185

"Do you think so?" she asked.

"It wouldn't surprise me at all," the old lady declared.

"But he seemed fond of Bettina and very upset last night. So did Jeri."

"I don't put any stock in public show," was Madge Carter's reply. "I always said there was something weird about those three. Why I sold them that property I'll never know."

Nina knew it was useless to argue with the old woman. Once she'd made up her mind there was no changing it. After breakfast she picked up her raincoat and escaped from the old mansion without encountering anyone else. This suited her well since she didn't feel in a mood yet to talk to anyone. There were so many things she needed to think out.

She avoided the pool and, without really intending to, began walking through the thick mist in the direction of the cottage and barn studio. Her mind was so filled with the tragedy and the other tormenting questions that she was hardly aware of her surroundings.

At last she neared the summerhouse and to her surprise she saw a bonfire burning in the field behind the barn and lanky Val Cramer standing by it. She walked a little faster and came up close to the fire just in time to see the young man lift up an effigy of Bettina and toss it into the flames!

Chapter Eleven

"What are you doing?" she cried.

Val Cramer turned to study her with contempt on his bearded face. He said, "Jeri asked me to do it."

Nina stood there gazing at the effigy which was rapidly being consumed by flames. She had a last brief glimpse of Bettina's features and then all was lost in flames and smoke.

She turned her gaze from the fire to the artist. She said, "It was part of your work. You shouldn't have destroyed it."

His Lincolnesque mask wore a bitter look. "It's what Jeri wanted," he said. "Bettina is dead."

It made no sense to her and yet she had an idea there was logic in it for him. This made her wonder if the burning of the dead woman's effigy had something to do with his purported witchcraft practices.

She said, "I hear the burial is to be on the island."

He nodded. "In the Dark Harbor cemetery."

"How is Jeri?"

"She's still in a kind of shock," Val Cramer said. "She and her mother were close."

"I'm sure of that."

He gave a deep sigh. "I must go back to her."

"Would she like to see me?" Nina asked.

He gave her a bleak look. "No," he said. "Not now. She doesn't want to see anyone." And he turned and strolled slowly back to the cottage.

She watched him go and then gazed at the bonfire for a moment. It was burning itself out and all traces of the blonde woman's effigy had vanished.

She stood there in the thick, gray mist with a feeling of desolation. She was no closer to clearing Grant's name than she had been months before. It began to seem like a lost cause.

Slowly she retraced her steps across the wet lawn. When she reached the old mansion she went inside and found Mort Venn standing in the living room. He was wearing one of the sporty plaid suits which made him look even stouter than he actually was. Seeing her enter the room he gave her a doleful glance.

"Not very good weather for strolling," he commented.

"No," she said, taking off her raincoat and seating herself in a tall-backed chair near where he was standing.

"Where were you?" The eyes behind the horn-rimmed glasses were questioning.

"I walked over to the Cramers."

"Oh?" he sounded interested. "And what was happening over there?"

"Something rather strange," she said. "I arrived just in time to catch Val burning Bettina's effigy in a bonfire."

The big man gasped. "He was doing that?"

"Yes."

"What was his reason for doing it?"

She raised her hand in a resigned gesture. "He claimed that Jeri asked him to do it. That she couldn't bear having a likeness of her mother around."

"A good excuse," Mort said grimly.

"Why do you say that?"

The big man shrugged. "I think it has something to do with the black magic he's been dabbling in. Bettina is dead and so he burned her effigy."

She stared down at the carpet. "I don't know."

"I can tell you one thing," the big man declared. "I've had enough of Pirate Island. I'm leaving the first of the week. What about you?"

"I haven't made up my mind."

He frowned at her. "If I were in your place it wouldn't take me long to do it."

"I keep hoping maybe something will turn up. Some new bit of information which will be the key to clearing Grant's name and Elise's."

Mort's face grew serious. "That's not going to happen and you'd better get used to it."

She looked up at him. "How can you say that with such certainty?"

"Because I think Grant and Elise were guilty as well as being lovers," he said harshly. "I've tried to hide my feelings from you before because I know how it was with you and Grant. But I can't see any point in lying to you about what I think any longer."

Nina was shocked by his words and put them down to the general state of despair they were all experiencing on this gray day. She said, "You can believe what you like and so will I."

The stout man said, "You're going to let yourself in for a lot of pain."

"Perhaps."

"I can only warn you," Mort said. "Grant wasn't worthy of you. He's better off dead. And you should let things rest as they are."

"I can't," she argued.

"Then I can't help you," Mort answered. "Not if you insist on being stupid."

"You'll simply have to do what you think is right," she said in an even voice. "But I know there is something strange going on here."

"You're talking about the Cramer's black magic?"

"No. Something different from that."

"What?"

"The ghosts I've been seeing."

Mort looked annoyed. "If you've been seeing these phantoms you talk about I blame that Val Cramer and his effigies. He's up to something."

"No," she argued. "You remember I saw Grant's face one night by the pool."

"Probably your imagination."

"It wasn't," she protested. "I know that I saw him. And I saw him again last night."

Mort looked astounded. "You saw Grant's ghost a second time?"

"It had to be," she said. "I was standing on the main street of Dark Harbor and I saw him standing in the fog on the steps of the Gray Heron Tavern."

"A likely story!" Mort said with sarcasm.

"It's not a story," she protested. "I did see him. It wasn't Greg, he tells me he didn't leave the house last night. So it had to be Grant's ghost, probably wanting to reproach me for not clearing up the scandal darkening his memory."

"Nonsense!" the advertising man scoffed.

"I saw him as clearly as the fog would allow and so did Derek Mills," she told him. "And when we asked for him they claimed there had been no one on the steps. Isn't that proof we saw a ghost?"

"Not for me," the big man said.

They were still talking when Kay Dunninger came in to join them. She showed the strain of the previous night and her black dress made her look even more pale and depressed.

Mort eyed her and said, "What's the idea of wearing mourning? You weren't related to Bettina."

The dark-haired girl looked shocked. "I had this black dress and I think it only proper to show some respect."

"You beat all!" the big man said.

Nina told her, "I think it's a nice idea. There's nothing wrong with it."

"Thank you," Kay said gratefully. She turned her back on Mort Venn and continued to talk to her, saying, "We've been informed that Bettina's funeral will be tomorrow. Mr. Carter thinks we all ought to attend."

"I'll be there," Nina promised.

"I never go to funerals," Mort Venn sputtered. "I didn't even attend Elise's."

"Surely you can make an exception for Greg's sake," Kay said.

"Greg isn't my guardian!" Mort snapped.

Kay turned to him with a disapproving look. "You can do what you like. I've delivered the message."

"I'm sure we'll all be glad when it's over," Nina said.

"I know I will," Kay agreed. "Funerals and deaths always upset me."

"Sentimental nonsense!" Mort declared and left the room.

When he'd gone, Kay said with distaste, "I'm afraid Mort Venn has no feelings."

Nina smiled grimly. "People in his profession aren't noted for them. They are practical men."

"He's a little too down-to-earth for my taste," Kay complained. "No wonder his wife turned from him!"

Nina's eyebrows lifted. She found this statement of more than passing interest. She had always felt that as Grant's secretary Kay must have seen and heard more than she'd ever divulged, but the plain, dedicated secretary was discreet to a fault. Perhaps now that Mort had upset her she might come out with something.

She said, "Do you think Elise turned away from him?"

"Yes," Kay said bitterly. "I'm sure of it. He had his girl friends on the side, you know. Yet he was always nagging her about Grant Carter."

Nina got to her feet. "What about Elise and Grant?"

Kay at once became wary again. She hesitated and then said, "I know that Elise was unhappy and Grant was sympathetic toward her."

"Just how much sympathy did he extend?" Nina asked with irony.

"I think their friendship was just that," the girl said. "Not the scandalous thing Senator Ryan and his crowd attempted to make of it."

"Have you any kind of proof of that?" she asked urgently.

Kay looked unhappy. "Only my own impressions."

"Did you ever hear that land deal discussed by them?"

"No."

"Do you recall anything they might have discussed that would help to prove them innocent of wrongdoing?"

"After the papers printed those stories they were upset. But they were always careful not to talk about it when I was around."

Nina gave a disappointed sigh and told the girl, "You raised my hopes for a moment. I felt that you might have something valuable to tell me."

"I'm sorry."

"It's all right," she said. "Keep thinking about those days. Tell me about any conversations you remember which seem important. We might just hit on something."

Kay looked frightened. "I don't want to be dragged into any scandal."

"I promise you'll be protected."

The girl said, "I'll try to think of something. But I can't promise. And I don't want to make Greg angry."

"Whatever you tell me will be in confidence," Nina assured her.

Kay gave her word that she'd try to help. They parted with Nina feeling that maybe she'd hit on a new vein. That Kay could, if she got over her fear, offer her some solid revelations which might clear up that long-ago scandal.

The following day the fog lifted a little but there were heavy showers. Everyone drove to the cemetery in Dark Harbor in Greg's station wagon and Mort's car. The stout man unbent enough to agree to attend the funeral.

Jeri, Val and the minister were already at the graveside in the hilly cemetery behind the church. From it there was a view of the harbor. Nina noticed this as she joined the funeral party with the others from Blue Gables. The service was brief, but before it ended a shower began. As she hastened toward the station wagon with Greg she saw Derek Mills coming their way carrying an umbrella.

Joining them, he said, "Let me see you to your car. Or better still, join me. I've been wanting to have a chat with you."

She glanced at Greg and saw he was looking none too pleased. She told him, "Greg, you go on and look after the others. I'll drive back with Derek."

"I can't stand here discussing it in the rain," Greg said with a hint of anger and he strode away toward the station wagon.

Derek sheltered her with the umbrella. "I'm sorry if I caused any trouble."

"It will be all right," she said. "He'll get over it. I didn't know you were attending the funeral."

"I decided I should," he said. "A sad business."

"It surely is," she agreed.

They reached his car and when he was behind the wheel, he said, "It's noon. Shall we go somewhere for luncheon?"

"If you have time."

"I'm not due back at the museum until after lunch," he said. "Let's try that restaurant along the shore road where we went before."

"Fine."

He said, "This coming after your near drowning must have caused a stir at Blue Gables."

"It did," she agreed. "Greg was supposed to go to the mainland for a few days but he cancelled it."

"He would have to," Derek said.

The rain continued as they drove out of the cemetery and along one of the quaint side streets of Dark Harbor between rows of typical Cape Cod houses painted in various colors. They reached the main street, and as they passed the Gray Heron Tavern she saw the dour Matt Kimble standing at the entrance studying the rain.

Derek turned off into the shore road and in a short time they reached the restaurant. Because of the rain there were few cars parked outside it. They went in and were shown to a table with a window overlooking the ocean.

After they had ordered, Derek said, "I wanted to talk to you about Bettina's drowning because I knew you'd been planning to question her about the scandal."

"I had planned to do that," she agreed. "Her death was a blow to me."

He asked her, "Do you think it was an accident or something else?"

"Dr. Taylor said she died of drowning."

"That doesn't tell me what you think," he said shrewdly.

"I'm not sure," she said. "You remember the experience I had in the pool. And it was Bettina who found me and saved me."

"That's right," he agreed.

"I have a strange feeling her death was planned," she said.

"You mean murder?"

"I suppose that's the only term for it. I think someone wanted to prevent her telling me what she knew about Grant and Elise."

"You feel she did know something?"

"Yes," Nina said. "She was going to hold a séance with me, but her daughter interrupted us."

"Jeri?"

"Yes."

He said, "Then Jeri must know something. And she must have had reasons to fear that her mother would tell you too much."

"I think so," she agreed. "Jeri was on Senator Ryan's staff while her mother was working for Mort Venn. And Bettina had been assigned to Grant's campaign. I feel sure now that she leaked valuable information to Ryan's office through Jeri."

"Probably," Derek agreed.

"With Bettina dead I doubt if I'll be able to prove it. Jeri is very wary and her husband helps her evade any involvement."

"So you've come to a dead end?"

"I thought so until yesterday," she said. "Now my hopes are raised slightly again. I managed to get Kay Dunninger to talk a little. She was Grant's secretary and I'm certain she knows enough to help me prove my case. But she's the sort of girl who is terrified of her own shadow."

"And she doesn't want to cooperate."

"That's it. But yesterday she became angry with Mort

Venn and began to talk without realizing how much she was saying. I'm sure this may happen again."

Derek studied her forlornly. "And so you plan to stay here and keep trying?"

"Yes."

"I'm disappointed."

Her eyes widened. "You want me to leave?"

"No. But I want you to be safe and I'm sure you aren't as long as you remain on this island."

She said, "I have a feeling the answer is here. How can I leave?"

Derek Mills sighed. "I know how determined you are."

She gazed at him appealingly across the table. "Do you dislike me for that?"

"No," he said. "I like you far too much."

"And I think you are my staunchest friend here," she said. "I might not have the courage to remain without you."

"That worries me," he said. "You make me feel responsible."

"No."

He told her, "One bit of advice. I think you ought to stay away from the Cramers."

"You do?"

"I do."

"Why?"

He furrowed his brow. "I suspect there is something not right there. I don't know whether it's criminal or not. They're up to some kind of mischief."

"Such as raising up ghosts?" she suggested.

His eyes met hers and there was a sober look in them. "You're thinking about our seeing Greg in that doorway the other night."

"Among other things."

"Did you ask Greg about it?"

"He claimed he wasn't in town that night and hasn't been to the Gray Heron in ages."

"So that eliminates him."

"If he told me the truth," she said.

"Right," Derek said wryly. "If he did, we're left with either a ghost or an illusion. Nothing very solid about all this."

"That's the trouble," she agreed.

They finished lunch and he drove her back to Blue Gables. The rain had ended and the fog had cleared. He helped her out of the car and stood for a moment at the door with her.

"I want you to keep in touch with me," he said.

"I will."

"I mean this," he told her. "I'm really concerned about you."

"I know," she said with a small smile. "And I'm truly grateful."

The brown-haired young man said, "You know how to reach me at the museum and don't hesitate to call me at home after hours."

"I won't," she said.

"I'm almost always there in the evenings."

She couldn't help but ask him, "What is the word on your wife? Is she any better?"

His pleasant face grew somber. "She has recovered from her violent spell. The doctor has assured me she's in no danger for the present."

"I'm glad."

"It is a small relief," he said. "But I'm pained to think of her spending the best years of her life in that hospital. It's very sad."

"For both of you."

He shook his head. "I'm sharing only a small part of the

tragedy. It's my wife's grim fate which deserves the pity."

They said goodbye and she went inside. The downstairs rooms seemed deserted, and she went up to her own bedroom. She'd been there only a few minutes when there was a knock on her door. She went to answer it and found Greg standing in the corridor.

Coldly polite, he asked, "May I come in?"

She stepped back. "Of course."

He entered the room, still in the dark gray suit which he'd worn to the funeral. He crossed over and stared out the window for a moment before he said anything.

Then with his back still to her, he said, "So you finally got back?"

"Yes. We stopped for luncheon."

"How pleasant," Greg said, sarcastically.

"I found it so," she said quietly. "I'm sorry about leaving you in the cemetery, but I wanted to talk to Derek about something important."

Greg swung around, his good-looking face twisted with rage—the kind of rage she'd never known from Grant. He said, "I can't believe you had anything that important to discuss with him."

"I can't help what you believe," she said. "I'm telling you the truth and I don't expect you to behave like a foolish boy!"

"What about your own behavior?"

"I have done nothing wrong!"

"So you think," Greg said. "You're supposed to be here because you were so in love with Grant that you treasure his memory. You can't think of any other man, you're so interested in clearing his name."

"That's true!"

"I'm sorry," Greg said. "I'm beginning to doubt it when you keep running off with that married man."

Her cheeks flamed. "You're being unfair!"

He faced her. "Do you deny Derek Mills is married?"

"No."

"Well, then?"

"You know we're merely friends—there's nothing more to it!"

Greg smiled nastily. "I know more than that. I know that he carried on with a young girl from New York last year until it was the scandal of the island."

"I'm not interested!"

"I just want to let you know about it," Greg said. "People here have long memories. And when they see you in his company they are bound to think you are his latest romance."

"Then they'll be wrong!" she declared.

Greg stared at her in unhappy silence for a moment. It was evident that he realized he'd gotten nowhere with his accusations. Now he seemed ready to try a different ploy. He took on a pleading look and reached out for her.

"Nina, you know I'm in love with you. Why do you enjoy tormenting me, making me jealous?"

She took a step back. "You have no right to be jealous."

"You loved Grant," he said. "Why can't you love me? We have the same blood. I even look like Grant, and I was the one who first knew you."

"But you're not at all like Grant beyond the physical resemblance," she told him. "He was considerate where you are cruel. He was generous toward people, and you are mean. I'm sorry, Greg, I can't find any substitute for Grant in you."

He stared at her. Then he said, "Thanks!" and strode out.

She closed the door after him feeling shaken and angry at the same time. Greg would never take Grant's place in her heart, and she'd felt it necessary to tell him so once again. She'd tried to make it plain before in a kinder way, and he hadn't listened to her. Perhaps he would believe her now.

For most of the afternoon she rested. The old mansion was quiet except for the sound of pounding from outside. She went to the window and saw that the carpenters had arrived and had started to build the fence around the pool. Aunt Madge Carter had not lost any time.

When she went down to join the others at dinner, Madge Carter was in a talkative mood. The old woman was pleased about getting the fence started and she did not hesitate to compliment herself.

"I had Jenkins and his men here as soon as the rain ended," she said with an air of triumph.

Kay Dunninger asked her, "How long will it take to put up?"

"A few days," the old woman said. "It depends on the weather. If we get more rain it will take longer. But when it's done we'll not have to worry about intruders getting into the pool again."

Greg shot the old woman an annoyed look. "We all know how much more clever you are than the rest of us," he said.

Aunt Madge showed a haughty look on her flabby face. She said, "I shall accept that as a compliment, Greg, though I know it wasn't meant as one."

The meal seemed to last forever and Nina, who had said hardly anything at the table, hurried to get up and found herself in the company of Mort Venn.

He asked her, "Have you been hiding all afternoon?"

"No," she said. "I didn't feel well. I rested in my room."

"None of us feels well," Mort complained. And then after looking around the hallway to be sure that Greg wasn't within earshot, he said, "I saw you leave the cemetery with Derek Mills."

"It wasn't meant to be a secret departure," she told him.

"Maybe not," he said. "But I can promise you it started a little hum of gossip."

"I hope not," she said worriedly.

"This is a small island," Mort reminded her. "Everybody knows everyone else and everyone else's business."

"So it seems."

"Greg was in a rage," Mort added, a wise expression on his moon face.

"I found that out," she said grimly.

"And I was hoping you two would hit it off," the big man mourned.

"I wish you'd stop trying to be a matchmaker."

"I enjoy it."

"That doesn't mean you're doing well at it," she said. And as she had a feeling she had to get away from the old mansion for a while, she asked him, "Can I borrow your car for an hour or so?"

He looked surprised. "My car?"

"Yes."

"What for?"

She really hadn't decided where she wanted to drive yet. Any place on the island would do. Anywhere to get away from the tension of Blue Gables. The first person who came to mind was Captain Zachary Miller, so she said, "I want to drive over and visit old Captain Miller."

"Oh?" He sounded doubtful.

"Yes," she said. "I promised him I would."

"You smashed up your own car driving in the fog," he reminded her.

"You crashed into me," she told him. "Your insurance company has admitted liability."

He frowned. "Well, that doesn't matter."

"It's not foggy tonight," she said. "Just dark. Can I have your car?"

The big man sighed. "Oh, all right. I might have known you'd get your own way. You always do."

"Thanks," she smiled.

"There are the keys," he said, giving them to her. "Be sure you bring the car back without any damage and remember it starts hard."

"I'll remember," she promised as she left him.

Ten minutes later she was driving away from Blue Gables. The big man had been right. The car did start hard, but it was modern and equipped with every automatic device and so was easier to drive than hers had been. She headed in the direction of Dark Harbor and then drove straight to the side street where she recalled having taken the old man.

It was an extremely dark night without any stars. But her headlights were good and there was no fog, so she had little difficulty seeing the road ahead. When she reached the street where the Captain lived, she began searching out his house. It was at the end of the street on a fairly large lot. She spied the lights in his windows and brought the car to a halt.

She turned off her headlamps and left the car to walk along the path to the front door of the cottage. She'd not gone more than a few steps when she saw a movement in the bushes to the left. Halting and giving her attention to it she suddenly saw a face in the shadows—Grant's face!

She cried out and as she did, the face vanished and there were only the bushes. She took a few steps across the lawn to see if any hint of the face remained, but there was none. Trembling with fear she turned and hurried to the Captain's door. She rang the bell and waited.

It seemed an endless time before the old man appeared. When he saw her, his wizened features took on an expression of delight.

Captain Zachary Miller said, "I declare, this is a pleasure I never expected."

Trying to shake off her fright, she said, "You invited me to visit you."

"But I didn't think you'd take it seriously. Young girls are always making promises and breaking them to old fellows like me," he said.

"I don't break promises," she told him.

"Good," the old Captain said. "Come in."

The house was small but decorated and furnished in good New England taste. She sat down on a love seat as he trotted off to bring her back a glass of wine. "Mustn't give island hospitality a bad name," he said.

"Thank you," she said, sipping the wine.

He sat down opposite her and saisd, "You had a drowning at your place."

"Yes," she said, taking a second sip of the wine as she was still cold with fright from her experience of a few minutes ago.

Captain Miller seemed not to notice. He went on, "And you had a narrow escape from drowning yourself when you fell off that boat."

"I did."

"People take boats out who know nothing about them," the old man said indignantly. "I dare say Greg is an example."

"It wasn't all his fault," she said.

Now the old captain was giving her a closer inspection and he said, "Why, you're pale as a ghost and I declare you're trembling."

"I'm sorry," she said.

"You don't have to be sorry," he told her. "What's wrong to upset you like that?"

She stared at him nervously. "I saw something on my way in here."

"What?"

"Grant's face looking out at me from the bushes!"

"You saw Grant?"

"Yes. I'm certain of it. And it's not the first time. I saw him the other night in the fog on the steps of the Gray Heron Tavern."

"You did?" the old man asked her in an awed tone.

"Yes. I've seen both Grant and Elise. Their spirits seem to be restless. Otherwise why would they haunt the island?"

"No other reason," the old man said solemnly. "You know what I told you about bodies lost at sea. Their ghosts return. Any islander will tell you that!"

She leaned anxiously toward the old man in the quiet of his tiny but spotless living room. "Then you do believe that I saw Grant in your garden just now? That his ghost is here?"

Captain Zachary Miller nodded gravely. "I have to believe you, Miss Patton. You see I've seen his ghost just outside the cottage myself."

Chapter Twelve

Nina gazed at the lined face of the old seafarer, looked deep into the still bright blue eyes under the white brows which had seen so many places, and found herself awed by his solemn words.

"You have seen Grant's ghost?" she asked.

"Yes," the old man said. "More than once. And it's likely others may have seen it as well."

"They have," she agreed. "And the ghost of Elise Venn!"

Captain Zachary Miller shook his head. "I did not know her."

"She came here during the summers with her husband and stayed at the Carters," she said.

The old man listened with interest. "And she was the one associated with that scandal concerning Grant Carter?"

"She was," Nina agreed. "It appears simple enough if one is ready to accept spiritualism. Their ghosts are not at rest because of the wrongs done them."

"Probably," he agreed.

Her eyes were wide with concern. "What is going to happen?"

"I very much doubt if we can in any way shape the future," Captain Zachary Miller said in his dry, old man's voice. "Better to leave it to the phantoms."

"You think so?"

"I do," he said with a nod of his white head. "And I want

to especially warn you against placing yourself in danger. You'll do Grant no good that way. Your safety would be his chief concern."

"That's probably true," she agreed.

"I think you ought to leave the island," Captain Miller told her. "Let events shape themselves. I have a feeling the truth will come out in any case. There is no reason for your taking risks."

She listened with a growing wonder. The old man was advising her to abandon the quest which had brought her to Pirate Island. He had been one of Grant Carter's good friends, and yet he was asking her to give up the struggle to find the truth about the scandals and save Grant's good name.

She protested, "I feel I owe it to Grant's memory to try and prove he was innocent of wrongdoing."

Captain Zachary Miller eyed her shrewdly. "You're still in love with him, aren't you?"

Nina was slow in answering. Then she said, "Yes. I suppose so."

"Grant would be happy to know that," the old man said. "But are you being wise? You can't live in the past."

"I must until I clear his name."

"I disagree," the old captain said. "I think you are taking too much on yourself. Why don't you try to forget all that has happened and find some other young man?"

"Not yet."

"If you remain here, you may find it too late," he warned her. "What about Greg Carter? I understand he is interested in you."

"I don't care for him."

"How about this Mort Venn?"

She grimaced. "I've never thought of him as more than a

casual friend. There is a grossness about him which I can't stomach and I'm not referring merely to his physical size."

Captain Zachary Miller agreed, "He is overweight. I've seen him." Then he asked, "How about Derek Mills? You go out with him now and again, don't you?"

She blushed. "Who told you that?"

The old man chuckled. "When it comes to gossip Pirate Island is a small place. And I met you at his office once or twice."

"So you did."

"Derek is a fine man."

"I agree. But he has a wife."

"That could change."

She said, "I haven't really thought of the possibility. I like Derek, but at the moment I'm only concerned with Grant and having justice done to his memory."

Captain Zachary Miller sighed. "Leave Blue Gables. That's my advice. Get away from the island for a while. You'll find that most of the problems will work out."

"That's your advice?"

"The best I can give you," he said.

"And if I don't take it?"

He frowned. "I'd be afraid that something will happen. That one morning you'll be found dead from some sort of weird accident. Just like Bettina Wells."

"There have been attacks on me," she admitted.

"So what I say should make sense to you."

"It does but I can't benefit from your advice," she told him. "I'm dedicated to my present course."

"Then take every precaution," the old man said. "Be especially careful at Blue Gables."

"I will," she promised.

She remained talking with him a while longer, and then he saw her out to the car. He gazed at the bushes where she'd seen Grant's ghostly face and said, "No sign of phantoms there now."

"No," she agreed. "But I still believe what I saw."

There was a rather strange expression on the old man's lined face as he turned to her and said, "There is no reason why you should have any doubts."

He waited by the car until she drove away and waved after her, a lonely figure standing by his gate in the darkness. She drove the car to the main street and then headed it up the steep hill. There were lights showing at the window of the Gray Heron as she drove by it. She meant to drive directly to Blue Gables, but it was still relatively early in the evening and on a whim she headed for the barn studio and cottage occupied by the Cramers.

She suddenly felt a desire to talk with Jeri. And she hoped, now that the first shock of Bettina's death had passed and the funeral was over, the dark-haired girl might be in a more communicative mood.

When she reached the road leading to the structures she saw there were lights in the barn. She parked the car, got out and strolled toward the entrance door of the studio. From inside she heard the blaring music of a rock band and she recalled that Val Cramer used a small sound system of recorded music for a background when the tourists came. But she had never heard it turned up this loud.

Her curiosity aroused, she opened the door to the studio and went in. The din of the music was deafening inside as she walked down the black curtained corridor on her way to the workshop. She noted that the effigies which had stood in the alcoves were removed now.

When she opened the door to the studio, the impact of the blaring rock almost forced her back. She braved the racket to venture into the fully lighted workshop and was shocked to find it turned upside down. It was as if a tornado had struck the room and smashed everything in its path. Moving on she came to the doorway of the showroom beyond, and what she saw made her stop and stand frozen in disbelief.

The dark-haired Jeri had an axe in her hands and she was striking out wildly at the effigies which were set out all around the walls of the showroom. She was screaming as she wielded the axe, and in her frenzy many of the figures had already been destroyed. It was a terrifying spectacle!

Then Jeri saw Nina and stared at her wild-eyed, the axe poised in her hands. Thinking that she might be the next target for the axe in the maddened girl's hands, Nina quickly backed from the doorway. In the workshop again she sought out the record player and switched it off. At least now she might have some hope of communicating with the seemingly demented girl!

The change from blaring noise to silence was dramatic. And from the next room she heard Jeri call out drunkenly, "You!"

Risking a second appearance in the doorway, she saw that Jeri had dropped the axe and was standing forlornly amid the wreckage of her husband's work. It took only a glance to see she was under the influence of some drug. Her eyes were wild, and saliva dribbled from the corners of her mouth.

"What is wrong?" Nina demanded. "Why have you done this?"

Jeri stood swaying slightly in the midst of the destruction she'd caused. "He's gone!" she said in a thick voice.

"Gone?"

"Val," the dark girl managed. "Val's left me."

Now she began to understand and feel sorry for the girl. Taking a step further into the wreckage of the room, she asked, "Why?"

Jeri made an awkward gesture indicating the destroyed effigies around her. "I told him I'd had enough of this. His playing the sorcerer—I hated it all!"

"And?"

"He told me he was tired of me and he's gone!" Jeri said with the suggestion of a sob in her voice.

"I'm sorry," she said.

Jeri raised her head and attempted to focus on her with those weirdly-distorted eyes. "You don't care! You . . ." She never did finish what she was going to say for at that moment she collapsed in the wreckage she'd created.

Nina went to her and made sure that she'd only collapsed and wasn't dead. She was still breathing but unconscious. Nina left her and hurried to the phone in the workshop. She found Dr. Taylor's number and called him. Fortunately she got right through to him.

"I'm here at the Cramer's studio," she said. "Jeri has just collapsed. She's been taking some sort of drug. It gave her a high and then she passed out."

"I'll be right over," the old doctor promised.

And he was there within five minutes. For once Nina was thankful that the island was so small. The old man came in and examined the girl and looked grim.

Glancing up at Nina, he said, "I've seen this drug before when that hippie crowd was at the monastery. Best thing I can do is drive her back and put her in the hospital. I'll give her an injection to help bring her out of this when I get her there."

"Is she in any real danger?"

"I don't think so," he said. "What brought all this on?" He indicated the wrecked room.

"She and her husband had a quarrel."

"I thought they were very close."

"So did I," she said. "But it seems they fought over the effigies. She told him she was sick of his concentrating on them and dabbling in witchcraft."

The old doctor whistled. "So that's what he was up to. I always thought him odd. I'd meet him walking alone in the night."

"He told her he was leaving. As soon as he went she came here and did all this damage."

Dr. Taylor glanced around. "I don't think there's a single figure left."

"I'm afraid not."

"Maybe it's for the best," the old doctor said as he lifted the unconscious girl as easily as if she were a child and carried her out to his car. As soon as the doctor drove away, Nina turned out the lights in the studio and got into her own car and headed for Blue Gables.

It had been a night of revelation. She was confused by the number of things which had happened. First, she'd seen the ghost of Grant. Then she'd talked with the old captain and heard him calmly agree that he also had seen the young man's phantom figure. Then he'd warned her to leave the island.

On top of this she'd gone to the Cramer's studio in time to find Jeri at the peak of her drug-induced rage destroying all of her husband's work. She could only wonder what Bettina would have said had she been there to see what was happening.

She arrived at Blue Gables somewhat shaken. Only a few windows of the old mansion showed any light so she guessed that almost everyone was in bed. She recalled the bitter quarrel she'd had with Greg earlier and hoped that he was over it. And she wondered how they would all react to the news about the strange goings-on at the Cramers.

She parked the car out back and locked it. Then she

walked in the darkness to the front entrance of the ancient house. As she did so, she experienced a kind of uneasiness, a warning sort of fear, as if she were moving into danger. And she recalled that Captain Zachary Miller had selected Blue Gables as the chief danger spot.

Trying to shake off this feeling, she entered the house. The reception hall was in darkness, but a soft light showed from the wide living room doorway. As she crossed the hall, Mort Venn came to stand in the doorway.

"I've been waiting up for you," the big man said.

She went over to him and gave him his keys. "There was no need," she told him.

He glared at her from behind his horn-rimmed glasses. "I wasn't worried about you, I was concerned about my car."

"Thanks for being so frank."

"It seems you've been gone a long while. How far did you drive?"

"I saw Captain Miller and then I stopped by the Cramers."

He looked interested to hear this. "How are they?" he asked.

"You're not going to believe this," she said. And then she told him all that had gone on there, up to the doctor taking Jeri away.

"I always considered that Val crazy," Mort said. "And I had an idea they were both on drugs."

"I didn't," she said.

The stout man told her, "Because you weren't looking for it. You go around in a daze thinking about Grant and the past."

"You think that's wrong?"

"I think it's futile."

"Grant is still vividly part of my life," she said. "I saw his ghost tonight. And I'm not the only one who has seen it."

"Pirate Island is loaded with ghosts," the big man scoffed. "Who cares about one more or less?"

"I do," she said quietly. "What about Greg? Have you seen him tonight? We had a bad argument."

"So it was a night for arguments," Mort suggested.

"He was very angry when I left."

Mort said, "I sat and talked with him early in the evening. Just after you took my car. He didn't mention your having an argument with him."

"He wouldn't," she said. "He can be close-mouthed. But he's also sullen. I expect he'll give me a bad time."

Mort smiled grimly. "Are you afraid of him?"

"Sometimes I think I am," she said frankly.

"Then why don't you leave here?"

"You know why."

"Not a good enough case, believe me," he said. "Go back to the mainland and forget the Carters."

"I wish it were that easy," she said sadly. "The trouble is that it isn't."

Mort said, "So you're staying on despite everything?"

"Yes."

"Looking for trouble."

"If you prefer to dub it that," she said.

Mort sighed. "I'm fond of you, Nina, but I just don't see things your way in this."

"I can't expect you to."

"I'm pushing my departure up," Mort told her. "I've decided to leave on the ferry in the morning."

"That soon?"

"Yes."

"I'll miss you," she said. "I haven't that many friends on the island."

"I'm glad you think of me as a friend," the big man said.

"And I do hate to leave you."

"But you're going to do it."

"No choice," he said. "You know the pressures."

"Thanks for the car."

He smiled grimly. "At least it got you around to see some things happen."

"A strange night."

He turned and snapped out the lights of the living room and then returned to her. "I'm weary," he said. "I'll have to pack in the morning, so I'll need to get up early."

She told him, "I'll be sure to get up to see you on your way."

"No need," he said.

"I want to," she assured him. She was going to miss Mort despite the fact he often annoyed her.

Mort accompanied her to the door of her bedroom and lingered long enough to give her a rather clumsy goodnight kiss. She submitted to it since it was in a sense a goodbye. She went into her room and began to prepare for bed. By the time she was ready there wasn't a sound but the washing of the waves on the nearby beach. The old house was deep in sleep.

Though she was in a nervous state she was also weary, and within a short time her eyes closed and she slept soundly. How long she slept was a question. She awoke to find the room still in darkness and with the sensation that someone had just called her name.

She sat up in bed and stared into the shadows, wondering what had aroused this strange feeling. Then all at once from outside her door she heard a board creak and someone softly say, "Nina!"

The voice was female but she could not recognize it. Yet the sound of it sent a cold streak down her spine. She heard a board creak in the corridor again and an odd rustling sound.

Gazing in the direction of the door, she was startled to see that someone was shoving a letter under it.

She threw aside the bedclothes and quickly crossed to the door and picked up the sheet of paper. Then she went to the dresser and turned on a small light to examine the message. She recognized it at once as a letter she'd sent to Grant. It was a love note in her own handwriting!

But what phantom hand had so gently slid the letter under the door and why? Her immediate thought was that Grant's ghost must be responsible. Placing the letter on the dresser she made her way to the door and slowly opened it.

Staring into the darkness of the corridor with frightened eyes, she was unable to discern anything. But the empty shadows only served to heighten the eerie feeling that somewhere out there a ghost lurked.

As she stood there filled with fear, she heard a board creak further down the corridor to the right. Her heart began to pound and gathering all her remaining courage she slowly moved along the corridor in the direction of the sound.

She could hear her own nervous breathing as she peered into the blackness of the corridor, and yet she couldn't see anything. Then there was the sound of feet scuffling on the stairway leading to the level above her. She hurried toward the stairway.

As she reached the next landing she caught a glimpse of a ghostly figure moving swiftly along the attic corridor. And the flowing white robe and streaming yellow hair left no doubt in her mind it was the fugitive ghost of Elise.

She had no intention of turning back now. If Elise had some message for her, then she must follow the phantom. She had delayed too long! Reaching the door which led to the captain's walk on the rooftop, she raced up the steps and came out to the walk and the cold dark of the night.

And standing facing her was the ghost of Elise. The spectre backed away as Nina gazed at her in stricken horror. There was something strange about the phantom. It did not look like Elise!

But before she could give any further thought to this, she heard a low, diabolical chuckle directly behind her. She whirled around in a panic to find herself looking into the grim, smiling face of Mort Venn. The big man stood menacingly between her and the door leading back down into the attic.

"You!" she gasped.

"That's right, Nina," Mort Venn said. He had removed his glasses and without them his face appeared truly cruel.

She swallowed hard and glanced toward the phantom Elise who was backed against the railing of the captain's walk, a flimsy ornamental railing.

Turning to Mort again, she said, "Who?"

"You need never know," the fat man said. "Tonight we're going to get rid of you for good and all. You're becoming a nuisance to us, Nina."

Staring at him accusingly, she said, "You were the one! You managed that land deal and framed Grant."

"I don't mind your knowing that now," he gloated.

"And she helped you!"

"Why not?"

"You played Grant's friend and betrayed him!"

"It's happened before," Mort Venn assured her. "And now you are going to commit suicide."

"Never!"

"You've a broken heart and a sick mind," Mort told her. "And it's over the railing!" As he finished speaking, he pounced on her and placed a massive hand over her mouth to stop her from screaming for aid. She knew she had little chance of defending herself against him, but the moment his hand went over her mouth she managed to bite it—and bite it hard.

Mort let out a howl of pain as he attempted to propel her to the railing and push her over the side to her death. He took his hand away from her mouth momentarily. At the same time she reached up with her free hand and scratched the side of his face. She could feel her nails catching under his skin and the warm trickle of blood as it followed her hand down the full distance of his cheek.

He cursed and hurled her roughly toward the railing. She almost went over but caught the top rail and her weight was not sufficient to snap it. He saw that she'd escaped death and came at her like a mad bull. She waited until the last moment and then dodged and hurled herself at his feet. He gave a cry of surprise as she gripped him tightly around the knees so that he completely lost his balance.

His heavy body crashed against the railing, and with a frenzied scream he plunged over the side. Nina had gripped his knees so tightly she almost went over into the dark chasm with him. She lay sprawled on the floor of the captain's walk for a moment gazing dully at the open space left by the broken railing.

"You vixen!" came a shrill voice of fury behind her.

Not prepared for this, she struggled to her feet as the blonde phantom who had lured her up there sprang at her.

Their duel was as fierce as the one just ended. This time her opponent was female, wiry and capable of inflicting more punishment than Nina could return. She also had the advantage of being fresh for the battle while Nina was already weary.

The two rolled back and forth on the floor of the captain's walk, the blonde phantom attempting to force Nina over the side. The strength of the blonde and the curses which streamed from her lips struck fear in Nina.

Then as she made a determined attempt to throw the blonde off her, the phantom's wig slipped and Nina at once recognized Mort's fellow-conspirator who was now trying to complete the task of killing her. It was Kay Dunninger!

Kay's plain face was ugly now, distorted with rage. She gasped, "You will die!" And she grasped Nina's shoulders again in a fresh attempt to push her through the break in the railing.

Nina felt herself losing ground and edging toward the side. She had about given up hope when she saw the shocked face of Greg looming above them. He swooped down, grasped the maddened Kay and held her struggling in his arms while Nina crawled back to safety.

Kay, realizing she'd lost, broke into tears and became the spineless, mousy person she'd been until the interlude on the roof. Greg roughly shoved her down the stairs before him and Nina followed. When they reached the first landing, she had the most devastating shock of the evening. Hurrying toward them from the dark corridor came a second Greg. It was then that she collapsed. . . .

When Nina opened her eyes she was on a sofa in the sewing room. Aunt Madge Carter in a blue kimono was bending over her with a worried look on her aged face.

"Are you feeling better?" the old woman asked.

"Yes," she said dully, "I think so."

"Your face is all scratched and bruised," Aunt Madge complained. "What a dreadful creature that Kay is!"

Memory came flooding back and she raised herself up on an elbow. "Where is she now?"

"They have her in the living room," the old woman said.

"They're waiting for the police."

"And Mort?" she closed her eyes and shuddered.

"He's on the asphalt just outside the front door. Not a decent sight for anyone. The gardener has put a sheet over him until the police arrive. You're lucky you're not stretched out there with him. That is what he and Kay were after from all I understand."

"Yes," she said in a small voice. "At the end I became very confused. I was seeing Greg double. Then I fainted."

"I know," the old woman said with a strange look on her pale face.

"It was Kay and Mort!" she said. "Why didn't I guess earlier?"

"We all should have," Madge Carter said. "And I expect they had something to do with that Bettina Wells woman drowning."

"I'm sure of it," she said. "She knew too much and they had to silence her."

"Something like that," Aunt Madge agreed.

At that moment Greg appeared in the doorway. He showed the strain he'd been under. His face was grim, but when he saw that she was sitting up his expression brightened.

Aunt Madge moved to the door. "I'll leave you two alone to talk," she said.

Greg came slowly toward her and then knelt beside the sofa and took her hand. And the instant his hand touched hers she knew! Her eyes widened and she gasped, "You're not Greg!"

He smiled and it was Grant's smile. "I'm glad you knew," he said. And he took her in his arms for a long moment. When he released her, he said, "I didn't know how to tell you."

She was confused and tears of happiness blurred her eyes. "How?"

"I came out of the wreck without a memory," Grant told her. "No one recognized me as the survivor of the accident. I wandered from village to village and managed to live a day at a time."

"How did you get here?"

"I rode on the ferry as a passenger. I was without purpose. I'd just a notion I wanted to reach Pirate Island for some vague reason I couldn't remember. I didn't know my name and by that time I'd grown a beard which hid my identity. I earned enough as a handyman to pay my way."

"Then what?"

"It was Dr. Taylor who first recognized me. He took me into his place and treated me and gradually my memory returned."

"Why didn't you let me know?"

Grant looked ashamed. "I should have. But I felt the best way of proving my innocence was to remain dead. That way the guilty would be put off guard. I was doing fairly well building a case for myself until you entered the picture."

"I was trying to do the same thing," she said.

"But you complicated the situation by making yourself a target for the criminals. Mort and Kay in this case."

"I didn't know!"

"Of course you didn't," he said. "I kept out of sight as much as I could. But I had others working for me, going through legal documents in Boston and all the rest. Gradually I realized that it was Kay who had betrayed me and that she'd done it for Mort."

"And Elise must have found out!"

"She did and they killed her and made it seem a suicide. Just as they did with Bettina because she'd guessed some of the facts about their guilt. And tonight was to be your turn."

She smiled at him. "They didn't count on your resurrection."

"I was at the Captain's," he said. "You caught me watching you from the bushes. After you left, the captain and I had a chat and I began to worry about you. I decided to come here. Something gave me the feeling that tonight might be the critical one."

"And it was."

"Mort's paid for what he did," Grant said. "And Kay will face a long prison sentence. She's broken completely and is ready to confess to falsifying the records in my office."

She suddenly remembered, "Tonight they lured me up there by shoving a letter I'd written you under my door."

"We must have a look at that," he said.

And they did a short while after the police took a hysterical Kay into custody. Grant found the letter on the dresser where Nina had left it and carefully read it over. Then he glanced at her.

"Clever," was his comment.

"What do you mean?"

"This was written as a love letter but there are sentences in it that could be construed as a suicide note. Especially as they were convinced that I was dead. This line would have backed up your suicide nicely, 'Grant, I have decided I can't live without you!' It fitted very neatly. And they almost managed it."

"Almost," she said in a hushed voice.

So Nina's adventures on Pirate Island were drawing to an end. The next morning she and Grant prepared to return to Boston. A sullen Greg had already left for the mainland. He'd turned out to be no better a loser the second time than he had the first.

When they drove down to the ferry the mists of Dark Harbor had settled over the island and the ocean once again. Dr. Henry Taylor and old Captain Zachary Miller waited in the dense fog to see them off. The Doctor had news about Jeri Cramer. "She's herself again and shocked by the news about Mort and Kay. She now wants to sell her place and leave the island."

Grant said, "Aunt Madge discussed that with me this morning. She's decided she wants to buy back the property." He turned to Nina with a smile. "She plans to give us the cottage for a wedding present. Says she wants us to come to the island but she knows you'll never want to stay at Blue Gables again."

Nina smiled in return. "Aunt Madge is a smart lady. I like the cottage idea. And I won't mind looking at Blue Gables from a distance."

Old Captain Miller offered her a calloused hand. "Don't be a stranger to Dark Harbor," he said. "I think from now on you'll enjoy it here."

"I've always liked the island and its people," she said. "Even the fog!"

The old man chuckled. "As long as we don't get too much of it. One thing more. Derek Mills phoned me this morning and made me promise I'd say goodbye for him. He asked me special."

She felt a moment of tender sadness. "That was kind of Derek. I'm very fond of him."

"I know," Captain Zachary Miller said with a wise look on his old face.

"Tell him I wish him well and that I'll be back," she said.

"I will," the old man promised.

Then the ferry gave its last warning blast and they said hurried goodbyes. She and Grant stood in the bow of the ship as it slowly made its way out in the fog. The outline of the shore became lost in the mist, just as all that had happened would vanish in the mists of time. But as she felt the warm squeeze of Grant's hand on hers, she knew she would always remember.